Ignatii N. Potapenko, William F. A. Gaussen

A Father of Six and an Occasional Holiday

translated from the original by W. Gaussen

Ignatii N. Potapenko, William F. A. Gaussen

A Father of Six and an Occasional Holiday
translated from the original by W. Gaussen

ISBN/EAN: 9783337287603

Printed in Europe, USA, Canada, Australia, Japan

Cover: Foto ©Andreas Hilbeck / pixelio.de

More available books at **www.hansebooks.com**

A FATHER OF SIX.

PSEUDONYM LIBRARY

THE
PSEUDONYM LIBRARY.

Paper, 1/6; *cloth,* 2/-.

И. Н. ПОТАПЕНКО

A FATHER OF SIX

AND

AN OCCASIONAL HOLIDAY

TRANSLATED FROM THE ORIGINAL

BY

W. GAUSSEN, B.A.

LONDON

T. FISHER UNWIN

PATERNOSTER SQUARE

M DCCC XCIII

A FATHER OF SIX.

" AH, martyr, long-suffering
martyr that I am! God is
gracious to others. Look at the
deacon of Perekopski, for example; the Lord was pleased to
call two of his children to Himself in one week. . . . Why,
what is the matter with you?
Tell me."

"Natiónka, Natiónka, the Lord
have mercy on you! what are
you saying? It is a sin even to
think of such things, but to say
them . . ."

Natiónka was lying huddled up
on a short, clumsy-looking sofa,
upholstered with green cotton
velvet with yellow spots. The
well-warmed room in which this
conversation was going on had a

low, somewhat sloping ceiling,
and little windows with uneven
panes of greenish glass, giving
the rays of light which penetrated
them a melancholy greyish tint;
the atmosphere was stifling and
laden with smoke, but nevertheless, Natiónka kept shivering and
drawing Father Anton's worn-
out beaver cassock more closely
around her. An indescribable
turmoil · was going on in the
room, produced by six children,
the eldest of whom was seven
years old, and the youngest was
trying to crawl along the thread-
bare carpet which covered the
floor. The eldest child, Timoshka,
was playing at being a priest, and
was imitating the manners and
intonation of the incumbent of
the place, Father Pankrátii, while
his brothers and sisters were sustaining the various parts of the
lesser clergy and the parishioners.
Somehow or other, the *rôle* of
tuitar,[1]   which   was   being

---

[1] Clerk.

played by the four-year-old boy,
Sasha, was unsuccessful, in consequence of which he received a
severe box on the ear from the
little five-year-old villain, Vaska.
Sasha's elder sister, Marínka, a
girl of six years old, with a pale
face and thoughtful expression,
interceded on his behalf. Marínka
was in her turn attacked by Timoshka, and a general uproar
ensued, and the various aggrieved
parties went for consolation to
the short sofa. Natiónka, whose
head was splitting and bones
aching, had to get up every
minute and administer justice
and quell the disturbance. All
this, of course, worried and almost
distracted her.

Father Anton, in the meanwhile, remained seated at a small
table, his back turned to his wife
and family, leaning his body
heavily over the table, on which
his elbows were spread out, and
was busily engaged writing up the
parish register book. The arrival

of the *blagotshínii* [1] was daily expected in the village, and this dignitary might at any moment express a wish to inspect the parish register book, and Father Anton had got behindhand with his work in consequence of his wife's illness. It was, moreover, of vital importance for him that the *blagotshínii* should find everything in good order.

Father Anton was in a desperate hurry—so much so, that he left his wife shivering from her feverish chill under his beaver cassock without even asking whereabouts her pain was, or how she felt.

The church could be seen through the little square window, and the space in front of it, with a glimpse of the frozen river beyond, whose surface was covered with an even layer of freshly-fallen snow glittering in the sun. A peasant, dressed in a patched cloak, a grey hat, and

[1] Inspector or superintendent of parishes for a district of the diocese.

high boots, was crossing the ice on the river, carrying a bundle of freshly-cut reeds. A miserable-looking horse was walking easily along the smooth road, and the wooden runners of the sledge to which it was harnessed, with their ends curved upwards in front, seemed to move along of their own accord.

"You had better let the children go out, Natiónka. Let them play in the snow. The weather is beautiful now," said Father Anton, continuing to write without altering his position.

"Ah, yes, let them go out! Let the earth swallow them up! Anything for a moment's peace!" exclaimed Natiónka, in a suffering tone of voice, flinging herself over on the other side, with her face towards the back of the sofa.

Father Anton shook his head and remained silent. "The Lord have mercy on her! what words!" thought he. "It is her illness that thus speaks; she herself does not really think this. Na-

tiónka is a good creature. . . . .
Ah, poor thing ! "

And he then began to wonder
how Natiónka could be cured of
the illness which had come upon
her,—God knows how! The
country surgeon had been to see
her, and given his opinion that
it was a fever. But this fever
had been going on for the last
two years. Natiónka would go
about for three days or so, and
then take to her bed for perhaps
a week. Even when she was on
her feet, she was struggling all
the time against her illness, and
in great pain. She used to complain of her chest and of pains in
her bones. The Lord only knew
what was the matter with her!
Father Anton consulted a certain distinguished physician in
the neighbouring town. But
this physician could not come so
far as their village, he had not
time ; and it was far to the town
—forty versts—and therefore impossible to drag an invalid thither
during the winter time ; more-

over, it was impossible to per-
suade Natiónka to do so. She
said it was nothing more than a
slight cold, which would pass off
when the spring came. The
country surgeon gave her quinine
powders, which did no good, and
only made her head ache. There
was also a peasant woman who
gave her certain roots and told
her to make an infusion of them,
and drink it every Monday and
Friday. This likewise did no
good. Perhaps when spring
came on, and the sun's rays
became warm, she would get
better. Then the children worried her a great deal; when-
ever she wished to get to sleep,
they would come and torment
her. Thus it was that she would
forget herself, and say things
that it was not in her nature to
say. There was no one to relieve her of her family duties.
Father Anton's sister was not
often with them. She stayed in
turn with her various brothers.
Ought she not to be sent for

now ?   All their troubles arose
from poverty.   The parish was a
poor one, besides which there
was properly speaking, no appointment for a deacon there.
Father Anton merely held the
place of *diatchok*,[1] and received one-fifth of the revenues,
and had to live as best he
could.   After eight years of married life they had six children.
Father Anton was still only
twenty-eight, and his wife twenty-
six, so they might yet have
plenty more ; and the question
how they were all to be fed and
shod was becoming a pressing
one.   A solution of the difficulty
would be found if only the bishop
would have mercy on him and
elevate him to the priesthood.
Natiónka would then be able to
hire a woman to look after the
children, she would probably recover her health, the children's
education could be undertaken,
and careers would be open to

---

[1] Sub-deacon.

them ; at present they were de-
prived of learning, and nowa-
days a greater misfortune than
that cannot be imagined. If
only his lordship would have
mercy on him, all would be well.

A smartly-turned-out sledge of
town make, drawn by a pair of
horses, passed in front of the
little windows. Father Anton at
once recognised the sledge and
its occupant.

" H'm ! . . . Here is the *blagotshínii*. He has gone straight
to Father Pankrátii's," added he
aloud. " And the register is not
written up. But perhaps he may
not ask to see it. I shall go and
find out if he has not some news
for me."

The deacon rose from the table,
and having carefully scattered
sand over his writing, poured it
back into a glass pot, closed the
book slowly, and placed it on a
shelf.

" Get ready, children, to go out.
You, Timoshka, dress Pelágii ;
Vaska and Axéntka and Marínka

will pull Sasha along in the little
sledge. Look sharp!"

"But I fear that they will
upset Sasha!" said Natiónka, in
a feeble voice.

"Aha!" thought Father Anton,
"notwithstanding the dreadful
things she says, she is really afraid
of the children coming to grief."

"Oh, no; it's all right; my
Marínka is such a clever girl!
Don't you be anxious, Natiónka;
I will arrange everything. Try
and get to sleep . . . and you
will be better in the evening."

Meanwhile the children had
stopped playing, and were busily
engaged dressing each other.
They were all glad to get out
into the bright sunshine and
sparkling snow, and expressed
their feelings with piteous
squeaks, mixed with ecstatic
cries. Three minutes later the
scene of the turmoil was transferred to the space in front of
the church. Snowballs were flying in various directions, and the
delight of Father Anton's pro-

geny knew no bounds, notwithstanding their miserable clothes,
which were torn and patched in
all directions.

"How they are enjoying themselves!" exclaimed Father Anton,
looking out of the window as he
arrayed himself in his winter
cassock over his coat.

" Tell them not to go on the
ice; there is a hole there; they
are sure to fall into it," said
Natiónka.

" Don't you trouble yourself,
my dear; it will be all right.
Go to sleep, and you will wake
up much better. God grant that
the bishop may take pity on
us, and . . . eh? . . . our desire
. . . may be fulfilled. We shall
soon get things straight then.
You go to sleep, Natiónka, and I
will run round to Father Pankrátii; maybe that the *blagotshínii* will be able to tell me
something."

Father Anton stooped down and
kissed his wife on the forehead.

" Tell Mária to look after the

children," added Natiónka, following her husband with her
eyes. Father Anton went out
into the vestibule making an
affirmative sign with his hand,
and carefully closed the door
after him. He felt for the handle
of another door in the dark vestibule, and opening it, looked into
a tiny kitchen, where Mária was
busy with her sleeves tucked up
preparing the soup. She was a
young, healthy-looking, red -
cheeked girl, with an unusually
lively, jolly-looking countenance.
Her father was a sad drunkard,
and, thanks to his brutality, her
mother was permanently laid up
with a broken leg, and their hut
was always cold and empty; but,
nevertheless, Mária was always
jolly, and sang all day long, and
there was not a youth in the
village who would pass her without stopping to pinch her plump
arm, or pat her on the back with
the palm of his hand; and she
would reply to this with a scream
and then burst out laughing. As

the deacon entered, Mária was humming an air while she stirred the soup.

"Look here, Mária, keep your eyes on the children and see that they do not go near the river," said the deacon to her, adding in a lower tone, "and if any of them cry and get chilled, bring them into the kitchen, and don't let them go into the sitting-room. The *matóushka* [1] is going to sleep. Do you understand?"

"Yes, I hear; I am not deaf," said Mária, grinning.

The deacon again went into the vestibule, and feeling for a third door-handle, went out into the roadway. The road leading to the church and the pathway to Father Pankrátii's house were covered with a thick layer of snow. The smooth surface was only broken by the footmarks of the children's feet and the two parallel lines formed by the

---

[1] The wives of the clergy are called by this name, which means literally "little mother."

2

runners of the *blagotshínii's*
sledge, and the millions of tiny
crystals were glistening in the sun-
light. The frost was fairly severe,
but the sun's rays, piercing through
the frosty atmosphere, struck
pleasantly on the face and hands.

Father Anton plodded along
through the snow, and, turning
to the right, went straight towards the incumbent's house.

Father Pankrátii lived in the
church house which he himself
had constructed, and to do him
justice it must be mentioned
that he had built it well and
commodiously. Its external
architectural beauty was not
particularly striking, but it was
spacious, being more than twice
the height of any of the peasants' huts; it had an iron
roof, and more remarkable still,
the house was built of stone,
whereas the other inhabitants of
the village dwelt in mud huts,
only a few of the richer members
of the community having edifices
constructed of yellow clay mixed

with straw. Adjoining the house
were all the necessary out-build-
ings—stables, cattle-sheds, barns,
coachhouse—and a whole *dessya-
tine* [1] of garden, most of which
was planted with cherry trees,
and also a few apple and pear
trees. This all stood on church
land—that is, land set apart
by the community for the per-
petual benefit of the clergy—
and the buildings were erected
with church money, that is to
say, with money subscribed by
these same parishioners some
fifteen years back, destined
originally for the benefit of all
the clergy; but Father Pankrátii
found that on account of his
large farming operations the
whole of this house and its
belongings would be suitable for
him only, and therefore left his
subordinates to hire huts, without,
however, forbidding them to con-
struct houses for themselves
should they care to do so. The

---

[1] Dessyatine=about 2½ acres.

subordinates at first intended
to protest against this to the
authorities, but when they came
to take into consideration the
dozen huge stacks of corn and
four most enormous haystacks
standing in Father Pankrátii's
yard, two partitions in his gran-
ary filled with last year's corn,
five strong, dashing horses, almost
a herd of cows, a thousand sheep,
a covered *dilijan*, [1] an ordinary
dilijan, not to mention a one-
horse shay—taking all this into
consideration, and likewise the
fact that Father Pankrátii was
on excellent terms with the consistorium, the subordinates came
to the conclusion that it was
perfectly reasonable that Father
Pankrátii should occupy the
whole of the church house.

Father Pankrátii held almost
an unique position among the
clergy of his province. He was

---

[1] A special kind of conveyance, introduced into Little Russia by the
German colonists, and used by the
richer portion of the community.

a clergyman-squire, or, to be more correct, a tenant-farmer, for the glebe land was not extensive, some fifty dessyatines. Finding himself in a poor parish, Father Pankrátii had turned his attention to agriculture, and for the last twenty years had conducted operations on a very large scale, growing yearly not less than two thousand dessyatines of corn; and besides this, during the last few years he had taken over a whole property on a long lease belonging to a neighbouring squire, who had gone out of his mind, and left his property in a very encumbered state. His wife had died when still young, leaving him one son and one daughter, and it was after this event that he had turned his attention almost exclusively to farming. He threw himself heart and soul into this occupation, either from want of something to do, or perhaps from natural inclination. He had large transactions with the merchants of the government town, both Russian and Jewish, who were all on familiar terms with him, and came to see his granaries, to feel the wool of his sheep, and taste his cheeses. Father Pankrátii might often be seen in the town on market days doing business, either dealing in horseflesh, or making terms with a gang of haymakers, or seeing his corn sacks being emptied into the warehouses.

He liked to do everything himself, and was blessed with an ample stock of health and energy. He was now nearly sixty years old, and this active and flourishing old man as yet showed no signs of feebleness; indeed, his hair was only just beginning to turn grey. He might be seen walking about the market in top-boots, in a fur hat, without his cassock, the skirts of his caftan fastened up, discussing prices and bargaining with the various dealers ; or else in the back room of a *tractir*, [1]

---

[1] Tea-house, or eating-house, keeping spirits and wine.

which he had entered by the private door (to avoid scandal), in company with a corn, milk, or wool merchant, where he would discuss business and draw up contracts. The incongruity of these unclerical proceedings surprised no one, because all the inhabitants of the town had long since become acquainted with his ways.

Father Anton entered his incumbent's spacious yard. The *blagotshínii's* sledge was standing in the middle of it. The horses had been taken out of the sledge and put in the stable. The snow was swept up into a heap in the middle of the yard, and fowls, ducks, geese, and pigs were wandering about in all directions. At his arrival two huge dogs growled angrily and darted towards him barking furiously, but straightway recognising their man, they began to wag their tails and lick his hands. Father Anton approached the covered porch leading into the house. Entering, he found

a distant relative of Father Pankrátii, who kept house for him,
setting out eatables on a small
oak table. Two different kinds
of smoked sturgeon were set out
on plates, besides onions and
large olives.

" Good-day to you, Axinïa
Melentiëvna," said the deacon,
bowing his head towards her
several times, wiping his shoes
on the mat placed near the door,
and trying to detach the lumps
of snow attached to them.

" Hu-u-mm! . . . " exclaimed
Axinïa, sharply, and throwing
down a knife and fork on the
table, put her hands up to her
left cheek. " Shut the door,
please, Father Anton; it is so
cold, and I have a toothache! "

Father Anton hastily closed
the door.

" Can I see the Father
blagotshínii? " asked he, in a
friendly tone.

"You cannot imagine what
pain I am in with my teeth! "
rejoined Axinïa. " I have tried

all sorts of remedies, but nothing
seems to relieve it. Ah, what
suffering! At times I feel as if I
could lay violent hands on myself
were it not for the sin."

" You should try using incense.
Have you not tried it? It is a
very good remedy," said Father
Anton.

" Oh, no ; it makes the teeth
crumble away—I have tried it.
How is your wife to-day, Father
Anton, is she still unwell ? "

" Yes, poor thing, and I can
do nothing to make her better."

" Ah, Father Anton, God forbid that the mistress of the house
should be laid up in bed ! God
forbid ! And with all the children too. . . . But does she
complain of pains in her chest ? "

"At times, yes. . . . Her chest
seems as if it would break, and
she suffers from breathlessness."

" Hm ! . . . I tell you what I
think. Don't be angry with me
for saying so, but I think she
has consumption. . . . My husband died of it, and he languished

away for three years just in the same way."

Father Anton stared at her with a frightened look in his eyes.

"The Lord be with you, what do you mean ? Good Lord God ! . . ." and he even crossed himself—" Can I go in to see the Father *blagotshínii ?* "

"Yes, yes ; he is inside with Father Pankrátii."

Axinïa wiped away the tears produced by the strong smell of the onions with her sleeve, and Father Anton was moved by this gesture, for he thought her tears were called forth by sympathy for his sick wife.

Father Anton walked into the parlour, and finding no one there, passed on into the drawing-room. Here the figures of two typical Russian clerics met his gaze: they were both seated in comfortable armchairs near a round table.

Father Pankrátii struck one at once as a man of extraordinary

strength, energy, and independ-
ence. Of medium height, thick
set, by no means thin—both the
absence of corpulence and the
full-blown cheeks betokened a
life of plenty, contentment, and
ease. His large penetrating
eyes wore a look of self-confidence, and there was no trace in
them of uneasiness or servility
in the presence of his superior ;
his manner was simple and easy,
and was that of an open-handed
master of a house who is glad to
receive an honoured guest and to
offer him the best of all that he
has. His expression and manner
seemed to indicate some such
sentiment as the following one :
I receive you with respect just
because you are the *blagotshínii* and possibly a useful
person, but remember, my friend,
I can get along very nicely without you, if necessary I could
snap my fingers at you, for I
have a hundred thousand in the
bank !

Father Pankrátii's face was

hairy, swarthy, and harsh looking, and was tanned by constant
exposure to the weather. The
hair on his head was luxuriant
and fell to his shoulder. When
engaged in business affairs he
used to tie it up in a knot and
put it under his hat. Father
Pankrátii received his visitor
dressed in a caftan, not considering the occasion sufficiently
solemn for him to array himself
in his cassock.

The *blagotshínii* presented
an entirely different type of
person. Being a relative of the
bishop, he had received an appointment which did not exactly
correspond with his years.
He was still quite a young
man, and wore a short beard,
and the curly hair on his head
was not very long; his dress was
very correct and tidy. His small
white hand, which seemed to
have been made for the purpose
of being kissed,[1] appeared from

[1] It is customary to kiss the priest's
hand when taking his blessing.

under the tight-fitting sleeve of
the light-coloured caftan which
he wore ; his boots creaked most
modestly, and he himself seemed
to be a most gentle, delicate
individual.

This man, with his good-
natured blue eyes and his open
sympathetic countenance surrounded with golden - reddish
hair apparently of recent growth,
appeared incapable of injuring
any one, and perhaps this was
so. He spoke in good Russian,
which formed a strange contrast
to the extraordinary mixture of
Slavonic, Little Russian, and the
literary language with which
Father Pankrátii expressed his
thoughts. It was well known
that the *blagotshínii* had come
to this part of the country[1]
with the bishop from some distant northern province, and that
he was on intimate terms with the
diocesan, a fact which, of course,

---

[1] The scene of this tale is laid in
Little Russia.

added considerably to the esteem
in which he was held.

"Ah, father deacon!" said he,
smiling pleasantly at Father
Anton's apparition, "I was just
coming round to pay you a visit.
I am very glad to see you."

He stretched out his hand to
Father Anton, and shook his
hand after the worldly fashion.
He liked to consider himself a
layman, and openly gave out that
it was only in consideration of
the bishop's repeated requests
that he had consented to become
a priest.

"Sit down, Father Anton,"
said Father Pankrátii, drawing
up a chair with his foot.

He always addressed the
deacon in the second person
singular, except on occasions
when he was displeased with
him. His seniority in age and
position gave him this right;
moreover, he was very well disposed towards Father Anton,
whom he had known ever since
he was a child.

Both the men looked Father
Anton up and down, for our hero
was of unusual height. Added
to this, if one remembered that
he was most extraordinarily
thin, that he held himself perfectly erect, that his tiny head
affixed to a long thin neck was
profusely covered with a mass of
dark thick curls sticking straight
out in all directions, and that his
face, devoid of beard or mous-
tache, had small, almost childlike, features, it must be admitted
that Father Anton presented
indeed a strange appearance.

Having seated himself, he
cleared his throat, and, in his
feeble tenor voice, said—

" I saw you going past my
window, . . . and so . . . I
came, but I will not stay, I am
interrupting you. . . ."

" What ! have you come to
see me about your petition ? "

" Yes, yes ; what else should
it be, Father *blagotshínii* ? "

" Well, I have seen the bishop
and spoken to him about you.

. . . I can hardly say that he was much inclined to consent."

"Not inclined?" asked Father Anton, in a low tone of voice.— " Ah, well! he is not inclined, . . ." repeated he, this time probably for his own edification.

" He is a curious man, the bishop," continued the *blago-tshínii;* "only just fancy, he likes you ! "

"Likes me?" muttered Father Anton, in a tone of bitter scepticism.

" Yes, isn't it strange ? When I informed him of your desire, and laid your petition before him, he said—

" ' Oh, that tall fellow, I know him—I know him—he is a good young man and not ignorant ! I know him.'

" ' Why, your reverence,' said I, 'he manages the parish schools, and has organised them excellently, for his chief has no spare time to look after them.'

"I had to say this," added the *blagotshínii,* turning round to Father Pankrátii, who nodded his head to signify that he had no objection.

"Well, that is what I said, and he answered—

"'Ah! just so, I always looked upon him as a promising young man, I always liked that tall fellow. . . .'

"'Ah,' thought I, 'the business is as good as done now!' But all the same it wasn't, for he added—

"'Notwithstanding that, I shall not make him a priest.'"

"What reason had he?" asked Father Anton, in the same agitated voice, by no means satisfied with this explanation.

"You would never guess his reason. He says you cannot sing in tune. Once, when he was conducting service at the monastery of St. John the Baptist, he told me that you, Father Anton, were acting as second deacon and sang out of tune. When the choir was singing in the key of D it seems that you

began in the key of G flat, and
that the effect was so disastrous
that all who were present had to
hold their ears. . . . Was this
so or not, tell me kindly ? "

" Yes, it did happen, Father
blagotshínii! But how could I
help it ? It was the first time
that I had ever served with the
bishop, and they gave me the
part of second deacon without
any sort of preparation or prac-
tice, but straightway—' Put on
your ' *stichar* ' [1] and perform the
service.' You can imagine how
nervous I was. How could I
possibly hit on the right note !
You see this was quite an unusual event for me. But I know
all the rubric at my fingers' ends ;
indeed, the bishop himself has
examined me in that. . . ."

"Yes, yes ; so he told me.
He told me that you knew the
rubric well, and that he likes you
and will make you a priest, but
not at present. This is what he

---

[1] Deacon's vestment.

said to me : ' Let him learn to sing in tune. He is still quite a young man. . . .'"

"Ha, ha!" interrupted Father Pankrátii, who up till this time had kept silence. "It's all very well for him to argue, he has no children ;¹ but how can Father Anton, who has six children, think about learning to sing in tune? it's as much as he can do to see that he does not put his cassock on inside out!"

"Ah, yes, if it were not for the children!" murmured Father Anton, with a sigh—"if it were not for my children! . . ."

The conversation was broken off at this point. Refreshments were brought in, and Father Pankrátii assumed the part of host and offered the *blagotshínii* and deacon something to eat and drink. The *blagotshínii* explained that he was very

---

¹ Bishops are always selected from the ranks of the monastic clergy, and are therefore celibates.

hungry, and set to work on the
fish ; but Father Anton refused,
and sat sadly watching the
movements of the *blagotshínii's*
jaw—that same jaw which had
so lately transmitted the unpleasant news to him, was now
busy munching fish.

" I tell you what," said Father
Pankrátii, addressing his two
guests, " this is all rubbish ! I
believe that if only the secretary
of the consistorium could be in-
duced to whisper a word or two
into the bishop's ears, the difficulty would soon be overcome—
that is my opinion."

" I don't believe it ! " muttered
the *blagotshínii*, in such an
uncertain tone of voice that it
was evident that he did believe it.

" But I am quite sure of it.
Excuse me, Father *blagotshínii*,
but you are still a young man
and cannot know. I know it,
however, and know it very well !
It is imperative to go to the
secretary, but of course to go
with something. . . "

" I keep silence on matters of which I am ignorant," answered the *blagotshínii*, diplomatically, and swallowing a third glass of vodka made the natural transition from fish to sardines.

" Well, I tell you straight out without any concealment, that I went through all this same trouble when I was trying to get a place for my son at Doukhóvka. The bishop raised all sorts of objections : he was young, inexperienced, and frivolous—my son, too. . . . Well, I went off to the secretary. I told him my story and trusted to his influence, but to make matters more certain, I wrote it all down so that he should forget nothing, and handed him the envelope. He was no fool and understood at once, so did not open the letter in my presence. ' Very well,' said he, ' we will see what can be done for your son.' ' That's all right,' thought I ; ' he has only got to see what is inside the letter, and the result is certain.' And what do you think? I came again two days later; the announcement of my son's appointment was made, and the whole thing was settled."

The *blagotshínii* evidently considered it his duty not to encourage such conversation, and had hitherto pretended he was not listening. But at this moment he drank a fourth glass, and his tongue seemed to become loosened involuntarily, for he asked—

" Did you give much ? "

"That I shall not say. Everyone gives according to his means. I will only tell you that I overpaid him. He would have done it for less. He is a knowing fellow, that secretary! Oh, I tell you he is! Here have I been labouring away for the last twenty years with my own hands, legs, and head, and the result of it is only some 60,000 roubles [Father Pankrátii never mentioned the real sum], while this secretary after twenty years' work has managed to buy a house which cost 200,000 ! After that, will you tell me he isn't a cunning fellow ? "

" Ah, Father Pankrátii ! I could tell you a thing or two about him," said the *blagotschínii*, suddenly losing all control over his tongue. " Two seminary students were both trying for one place—it was a fine place. The first one came and left a packet, an hour later came the other and also left a packet. He received them both, but of course gave the place to one only. But the point of the story is that the one gave two hundred and the other three hundred ; well, of course, the second one secured the place."

" Did he return the two hundred ? "

" Not he ! Ha, ha, ha, ha ! I should think not, indeed ! "

" But what does the bishop say to this ? "

" Oh, the bishop ! " continued the *blagotshínii*, in a jovial

tone of voice, "what can he
know about such things? You
must consider his position. He
only views this sinful world
either from his reception-room,
where all his visitors come to
him as petitioners—of course, in
a most devout frame of mind—or
else from the windows of his
carriage, whence he catches
a glimpse of humanity, and
gives it his blessing, or else at
some public dinner, where he
sees people in dress-clothes,
wearing all their orders, or
finally on his pastoral visita-
tions through the diocese, when
he is met everywhere by the
clergy in their most spick-and-
span array. But it is hard for
the bishop to know real life as it
is."

"Yes, that is quite true, Father
blagotshínii!" said Father
Pankrátii, in a tone of convic-
tion, and the deacon sighed
deeply.

"Of course it is true! And I
don't mind saying who told me

so—the bishop himself, egad, it was. That is what he thinks. 'And we are powerless before this evil owing to our position. If only we were worldly people, we could know the world as it is.' Such were his words!"

The Father *blagotshínii* now began to feel that he was saying too much, and suddenly became silent. Father Pankrátii urged him to drink a fifth glass, but he steadily refused.

Father Anton got up from his chair.

" Well, Father *blagotshínii,* what do you recommend me to do ?" asked he, looking down at the dignitary's jovial face. The latter answered nothing, but only folded his arms and assumed an expression of doubt and per- plexity.

" You should start off to town and visit the secretary. That is the best thing to do," answered Father Pankrátii, on the other's behalf.

Father Anton took leave and

went out without any further
remark. " What injustice ! "
thought he to himself as he went
home. " He admits I manage
the school well, and know the
rubric, and all the rest, but
simply because I sang out of
tune. . . . Six children, good
Lord God! Hear me, your
reverence ! H'm ! . . . go to the
secretary ! But what is the use
of it ? He will never understand
if I tell him I have six children
and a sick wife. His heart is
probably as stony as all the
others. But what am I to say to
Natiónka ? Poor thing, she is
expecting to hear good tidings
from me ! Ah, me, alas ! what
am I to say to her, poor thing ?
It is impossible to tell the truth.
She would be upset and begin
to cry and curse her life. . . .
What an ill-mannered creature
that Axinïa is ? devoid of all
good feeling ! What a heartless
thing it was for her to say that
Natiónka has consumption ! . . .
How easy it is to say a cruel

word! and in such a brutal way! She is simply an ill-bred woman!"

Anton decided in any case not to tell his wife the truth.

On arriving at the space in front of the church, he found the children still playing there. They had made a huge snow-man, and Váska, in order to give the finishing touches to his head, was standing on a stool which he had brought out of the house. Marínka was not there. She had gone back into the kitchen to rock Sásha to sleep.

Father Anton took off his cassock in the kitchen, wiped his shoes, and after warming himself by the stove, determined to go into the parlour.

Here he found his wife dozing, but she opened her eyes immediately when he appeared.

"Well, what did the *blago-tshínii* say?" asked she; evidently she had been thinking of nothing else all the time.

"Oh, nothing special, Natiónka, he said that the bishop is favourably disposed towards me."

" That means he will make you a priest ? "

" Of course he will. . . . But only he said I must wait a little. . . . And he . . . said I must . . . present myself personally to the bishop. . . . He wishes to see me."

" What a wonderful thing! He wants to see you ? "

" I suppose so ; well, let him have a look if he likes, he won't make me any the shorter for that. . . ."

Father Anton, in order to enliven his wife, gave a little titter at this last joke. But terrible perplexity was in his mind. How was he to find money for his journey to town ? He had nothing left which he could either pawn or sell. What would his solitary jade or his old cow fetch ? At the end of the winter, when provender was scarce, no one would take them at any price. And then, how could he leave his family without milk? No, it was useless to think of that, and he was only deceiving his wife by vain hopes.

But Natiónka added—

"Well, I suppose, if you have to present yourself, you had better lose no time in starting. One must strike when the iron is hot."

"All right, Natiónka, I shall be off! I shall write to my sister Douniásha to come and look after you during my absence."

The deacon sat down and wrote to his sister, but was in ignorance of how he would find the necessary means for his journey to town, or what he would do when he arrived there. His chief anxiety was to make his wife's mind easy.

BOUTISTCHÉVKA was a large but miserable village. Its population increased rapidly, and new mud huts were constantly springing up, but why people lived here in preference to some more flourishing locality, no one, not even the inhabitants themselves, could say. The villagers possessed but little land, and this was divided up into small lots, which were totally inadequate for the sustenance of their owners. In days gone by, the river had been the chief source of wealth, but fifteen years ago the family who had owned the place from time immemorial had sold their property, which passed into the

hands of a certain merchant—
Skridloff by name—who soon
made good his claim to the river
with all its fish and the reeds
lining its banks, and sold the
right to the use of these pro-
ducts to the peasants at a ruin-
ous price. The moujiks lived
on their miserable allotments in
a state of permanent semi-star-
vation, and the population continued to increase with unfailing
regularity. It is sufficient to
say that the *kabatchik* [1] Jesse
found it unadvisable to drive
his claws any deeper into
Boutistchévka; and after due
consideration removed his " establishment " to an outlying de-
pendency of the village ten versts
off, called Tcherkin, where there
were twenty or thirty huts, which
belonged to well-to-do people,
who imbibed vodka in large doses.
Thus it was that a fresh

[1] Publichouse keeper — an industry
generally in the hands of the Jews, who
are allowed to live in this part of the
empire.

calamity befell the dwellers in
the luckless village of Boutistchévka ; they had to get ten
versts to satisfy their thirst, but
this circumstance in nowise di-
minished their ardour. Some of
them, indeed, found that the extra
journey improved the flavour.
But the majority deplored the
transfer of the " establishment "
to Tcherkin.   It had hitherto
been the one pleasant corner in
Boutistchévka, and life without
it, lost its solitary charm. Some
people had petitioned Jesse to
return, but nothing came of it ;
for Jesse founded his calculations on that infallible law of
political economy—supply and
demand.   The settlement of
Tcherkin demanded vodka, and
thither he took his supply. It
can well be supposed that, under
these   painful   circumstances,
there was no parishioner to
whom Anton could turn for
money to enable him to undertake his journey. It was absurd
to expect any help from the new

proprietor, the merchant Skridloff. The one absorbing pre-
occupation of this latter person
was to turn everything that
would fetch a copeck into money,
and used to lament bitterly
when his last lot of reeds
was sold and there remained
nothing else to realise money
upon. The only thing left to
Anton was to turn to his incumbent for a loan. Father Pankrátii, at any rate, knew him,
and would surely trust him.

This was four days after the
interview with the *blagotshinii*. The snow was melting,
and it hardly seemed likely that
any more would fall that winter.
Water appeared on the surface
of the ice on the river, and
people had ceased to trust themselves upon it any longer.

The beginning of March had
brought the first warmth of the
sun's rays, and almost a spring-
like feeling prevailed in the air.
The new grass began to appear,
and the birds chirruped more

confidently than before. Anton
told his wife that he had to take
the parish register to the priest;
but the real nature of his business was of a far more serious
nature, and he felt that he was
about to undertake an important step. In case he met with
a refusal everything would be
at an end, for there was no
one else to fall back upon.
There were, however, certain
indications which made him
view the situation hopefully.

He knew that it was only the
day before, that Father Pankrátii had sold his last year's
wheat very advantageously. This
should surely dispose the incumbent to assist him. Moreover,
he had recently received fees, so
that he could not refuse on the
score of having no ready money.

Father Anton started off on
his errand, buoyed up with
hopes. It was Sunday, and
mass was just over. The incumbent, who was drinking tea,
received his visitor affably.

' Will you have some tea,
father deacon ? "

" No, thank you, I have just
had some. I have come to see
about a little matter of business,
Father Pankrátii."

" Business? Well, let me hear
what you have to say."

" I wish to speak to you about
my prospects."

" H'm ! . . . how can I help
you in your prospects ? If only
I was the bishop, I would make
you a protopope straight off."

" Ah, it is not that exactly.
If you remember, you advised
me to go to the secretary. It is
no use to go to him empty-
handed. . . ."

" Well, of course we all know
that. What would he care for
your visit ? "

" That is just it. And as I
have no money . . ."

" If you have got nothing it is
no use your starting," concluded
Father Pankrátii with fatal logic.

" He does not understand me,"
thought the deacon, and felt at

this moment that there was little
to be got out of the incumbent.
But still he would try again.

" I thought . . ." began Anton, and then got confused
again.

" What did you think, Father
Anton ? " asked the other, whose
tone betrayed but little hope of
success.   " You thought, I suppose, that heaven would shower
down money upon you.   No, my
friend, there is no money in
heaven."

" Oh, no, I only wished to ask
you. . . . Will you take pity on
me and lend me money?   I
would repay you early in Lent."

" I have no money, my
friend," answered Father Pankrátii, shortly, without giving
any further explanation.

Father Anton was silent, he
was quite unable to understand
how people could refuse so abruptly.

There was no doubt about the
fact that the money which Father
Pankrátii had received the day

before was safe in his pocket,
and he himself had made no
secret of it; on the contrary, he
had even boasted of it before the
churchwarden. " See," said he,
" what I have just received ; I
kept my corn through the winter
and am a thousand roubles the
better for not selling earlier." And
then the same man unblushingly
declares that he has no money.
If father Anton had money in his
pocket and was asked for a loan
by some one—let us suppose,
whose credit was not very good
—he would doubtless have made
the most polite excuses for half
an hour, and would probably
have ended by giving the money.
To a downright " no," there is
nothing more to be said. Thus
it was that the last ray of hope
vanished like smoke, and Father
Anton saw that his last chance
was gone. But he must surely
have known his incumbent's rule
of never lending money to any
one under any circumstances
whatever. Occasionally a mou-

jik would implore him for thirty
roubles to buy a horse with, in
order to get his land ploughed,
promising to return it; but Father
Pankrátii always answered, " I
have no money." This was a
fixed principle of his. The reason of this was that, conducting
affairs of an unclerical nature on
such a large scale, he found it
advisable to avoid any action
which might make his conduct
appear in an unfavourable light.
This flourishing position had
. already earned for him plenty of
enemies, who, on the slightest
pretext, would have been ready
to accuse him of being a usurer
and extortioner.

Anton was well aware of this
rule, but thought that an exception might have been made in
the case of a colleague, under
such peculiar circumstances.
After a prolonged silence, Father
Pankrátii said—

" Perhaps my daughter Mariána Pankrátiévna may be able to
help you, she generally has some

ready money; you ask her, and see if she will. . . ."

"Mariána Pankrátiévna?" asked Father Anton; "but she is very exacting."

"Well, my friend, that's your affair. . . . Please yourself. . . . Maybe she will make easier terms for you! Anyhow, ask her; why, here she comes."

At that moment the priest's daughter entered the dining-room. She wore a long, checked morning-dress, which fitted her very badly, and was stained and worn out, and gave the impression of having been made long ago, when she was stouter and younger. This most probably was the case, because Mariána Pankrátiévna had led a dull, solitary life with her father, and had seen better days at a period when she was stouter and jollier. Although only thirty-five years old, she looked at least forty. Her long thin arms attired in loose sleeves, her emaciated hands, flat figure, swarthy yellowish complexion, and scanty hair, all betokened a dried-up person. She was a widow; her husband, a priest, had only survived his marriage three years, and died without leaving any children. From the time of her husband's death she had rapidly grown old-looking and lean. She would doubtless have been willing to venture on matrimony a second time, and owing to her father's wealth, had received more than one proposal. But her ideal was the clergy. She used to say to her suitors, " I could not become the wife of an official or merchant after having been a *popadyá*.[1] It would be like degradation from a general to the ranks." Such was the high opinion she entertained of the calling with which she had identified herself by her first marriage. But, unluckily, candidates for the holy office, as is well known, are forbidden to marry widows. Thus it was

---

[1] Priest's wife.

that Mariána rejected all her
admirers. Very possibly by this
time she had become less exacting, and might be inclined to
change her ideal. But suitors
were no longer forthcoming, and
she now considered herself a
widow for ever. She occupied a
separate part of the house to her
father, and never troubled herself
with his affairs. She had her
independent fortune, originally
amounting to three thousand
roubles, which was her marriage
settlement; and owing to her
business-like capacities, had
already turned this into fifteen
thousand. The peasants of the
village frequently visited her part
of the house, and rarely went
away without having transacted
their business.

"The deacon wishes to see
you on business, Mariána," said
Father Pankrátii. "I really
don't know what it is about, but
he will explain it to you." .

Having said this, the priest left
the room and entered his study.

Anton bowed to the priest's daughter, who did not hold out her hand to him, for she considered it beneath her dignity to shake hands with any of the lower orders of the clergy.

"What is it?" asked she, drily.

"I . . . eh . . . want . . . eh . . . to borrow some money. . . . I am in very difficult circumstances, Mariána Pankrátiévna— very difficult!"

"Money? From me? But why don't you ask my father?"

"Father Pankrátii tells me he has none."

"Well, supposing I have?"

"You have?" asked Anton, his face lighting up, as though it mattered not whether she would accede to his request or not.

"Yes; but my terms are very hard."

"I am in such difficulties that I shall be glad to borrow on any terms."

"How much do you want?"

"Altogether . . . eh . . . one

hundred and fifty roubles!"
Father Anton up till this moment had not thought about the
amount of the sum required, and
mentioned this figure more or less
at random, but the thought just
flashed through his mind, "I
must square the secretary with a
hundred, and fifty for expenses.
I must buy Natiónka a silk
shawl, and a doll's house for the
children."

"My terms are hard, Father
Anton. I am really sorry for
you."

"What interest will you re-
quire, Mariána Pankrátiévna?"
The deacon was boiling over with
impatience, and felt inclined to
agree to the most exacting terms.
"Once I am a priest, I shall
easily be able to pay it off again."

"To-day is the 12th of March.
You must repay me on the 12th
of April. Here is a hundred and
fifty roubles, and you will give
me back two hundred; and also
you will hand me the proceeds of
the sale of your winter crops."

"What do you mean?" ex-
claimed Father Anton.

"You have sown your winter
crops, I suppose?"

"Yes, seven dessyatines."

"Very well; you shall draw up
a contract to the effect that you
have sold your winter crops,
whatever they may amount to.
This is merely a security. I do
not want your crop. You know
very well I do not deal in corn."

Father Anton gazed at the
woman and wondered that such
people could exist in the world.
"And she is a *popadyá* and a
priest's daughter!" thought he,
"and brought up in the diocesan
schools. Good Lord, Good
Lord!" But Anton was more
especially surprised that he
should be thus treated. He
instinctively tried to fathom this
phenomenon. He knew of course
that Mariána did not accommo-
date the wants of the moujiks for
nothing. If she gave one of
them ten roubles in the spring,
she would take back twenty at

the feast of the Intercession.
But the moujik being a proprietor
of land, she required no security
of him. With the deacon things
were different, for he might be
turned out of his place at any
moment, or be transferred to
another parish.

Anton's hesitation did not last
long; indeed, what could he do
in such an extremity? So he
said—

"Well, hand me the money,
Mariána Pankrátiévna."

"So you agree to my terms?"

"I agree."

"My conditions are very hard;
I am indeed sorry for you."

"There is nothing else for it,
Mariána Pankrátiévna, I am in
very great straits."

Anton hastily concluded this
disgraceful bargain, fearing that
the priest's daughter might
change her mind and refuse to
let him have the money. Indeed,
his whole future prospects depended on his getting this sum.

Mariána, however, had no

intention of torturing his mind
with doubts, and a quarter of an
hour later he was at home again.
Natiónka had got up. She felt
better. Father Anton wished to
talk to her calmly, but could not
restrain the joy which filled his
breast. The thought that he had
a hundred and fifty roubles in his
pocket made him feel just as if
he had gained the ambition of
his life and was a priest with a
living of his own.

"I hope Douniásha will come
soon, as I want to be off to the
town," he kept repeating, and
often went out into the roadway
to see if there were any signs of
his sister's arrival. At length a
peasant's conveyance was seen
approaching, all bespattered with
liquid mud from the road, which
was covered with streamlets of
water from the thawing snow.
A peasant was seated on the front
part of it, and his legs dangling
in the air seemed at times to be
mixed up with his horse's hind
legs: behind him was seated

Douniásha, a handsome girl,
with a pleasant countenance, a
sonorous voice, and lively manners. She immediately set to
work to get her brother's house
put in order. Although totally
uneducated, she was an excellent
household manager, and incapable of remaining idle for a
minute.

Her four brothers—who were
all unsuccessful men, having
none of them attained a higher
rank than that of deacon—considered themselves lucky when
their sister paid them a visit.
She used to look after the children, manage the kitchen de-
partment, milk the cows, and do
the sewing ; in fact, she was worth
her weight in gold—about this
all her brothers were unanimous.
She had many admirers, but was
in no hurry to marry, for she
knew her worth and valued the
liberty of single life. "I am a
free bird," she would say, "and
flit from one brother to another
like a butterfly ; if I marry there

will be children, illness—and good-bye to the joys of life. I have seen enough of wedded life." Father Anton became much more lively when his sister arrived, and even his wife began to take a less hopeless view of the world in general.

"Thank you, Douniásha, for coming; I am off to the town to-day."

"We shall get on very well without you," retorted Douni-ásha.

A few hours later Anton was on his way to town. The road was in a most terrible state. His wretched jade kept stumbling over the holes in the road. Father Anton was all covered with mud. The horse walked nearly the whole way, so that the journey occupied all night. Scarcely a hut was passed the greater part of the way. On approaching the town, settlements and houses became more and more frequent, and towards dawn the town was at last reached.

Here the ill-paved streets were
literally a sea of mud, and foot
passengers who wished to cross
them seemed as though they
had made up their minds to
take a dive and swim for it.
Father Anton went straight to
the inn. It was still early
according to town reckoning—
seven o'clock. He wished to
wash and tidy himself up. It
was hardly likely that the secretary would get up till eight
o'clock, or that his office would
be opened earlier than ten. So
Anton thought it advisable to
visit him between these hours, and
having drunk tea, which refreshed
him after his night journey, he
procured a piece of notepaper
and an envelope. He wrote his
petition for promotion to the
priesthood on the paper, and
carefully folding it up with the
hundred rouble note enclosed
between the sheets, placed it
in the envelope. Anton did all
this with a look of boldness and
confidence, probably because he

was alone in a room at the inn,
and the stories related by his
incumbent and by the *blagotshínii* were fresh in his mind
and made him feel sanguine of
the success of his enterprise. It
all seemed such a straightforward, simple thing to do. At nine
o'clock he had already arrived
at the secretary's rooms, and was
waiting in the entrance hall.

"What am I to tell the secretary you have come to see him
about, *bátioushka* ?" asked an old
woman, who, to judge by her
appearance, might either be the
secretary's wife or housekeeper,
or else an old nun.

"Well . . . It does not matter
. . . he does not know me. I
have come to him about my own
business."

" I suppose you would scarcely
come about any one else's," and
the old woman disappeared into
a long, gloomy corridor.

Father Anton paid no attention
to the old woman's remark.
He was astonished by the sound

of his own voice, which now
sounded wonderfully feeble and
nervous. And after all, there
was nothing to be frightened at.
Like all other entrance halls,
this one was furnished with two
chairs, a table surmounted with
a looking-glass, and a row of
pegs to hang hats and coats on.
Through the half-opened door,
he could see into the drawing-
room, which was decorated with
handsome furniture in brown
holland coverings, and an instru-
ment of the harmonium tribe.
The old woman, too, did not
present a very striking appearance; everything was, in fact,
very much the same as in other
people's houses. But none the
less Father Anton found himself
prostrated by a desperate attack
of nervousness. The cause of
this must doubtless have been
that envelope in his pocket,
which enclosed his petition and
the bank note. What would be
the ultimate result of that hundred rouble note? It was either

to be his salvation, or else it would be the cause of his irretrievable ruin. The old woman soon reappeared, and invited him to follow her. Passing along the dark corridor, he turned to the left and suddenly found himself in the secretary's study. The room was a very small one with a low ceiling, two small windows looking out on a courtyard, and a clumsy-looking writing table, the green cloth of which was covered with ink stains. Above the low table in the corner of the room hung several *eikons*, or sacred pictures, and before the largest of these a lamp was burning. A smell of burning olive oil from this lamp pervaded the room, and the little flame twinkled and crackled. The secretary occupied hired rooms, and no one would have supposed that he was the landlord of a house worth 200,000 roubles. But this was so. Father Anton had seen this man twice at the consistorium, and

immediately recognised his face.
He was an enormous man with
a large head covered with grey
hairs, his face was clean shaven,
and as red as that of a man who
has just emerged from a cold
bath; his long black frock coat,
his broad, somewhat stooping
shoulders, gave his visitors a
feeling that their arrival was not
welcome. It seemed as though
he was indifferent to all mankind,
and was vexed at being disturbed
by visitors. He remained standing near the door, with his face
half turned away from his visitor,
as though about to sneeze.
Father Anton made a profound
bow to him.

"What is your name?" asked
the secretary in a boyish voice,
ill in keeping with his sedate ex-
terior. Something in the nature
of a good bass growl might have
been expected from a person with
so commanding a presence. In
addition to this, he drawled out
his words with somewhat of a
nasal twang.

" I·am the deacon of Boutistchévka—Anton. . . ."

" Boubuirko ? " interposed the
secretary, abruptly, motioning to
him to take a seat, and himself
walking with heavy steps towards
his armchair.

" I am he ! . . . I . . . the
Father *blagotshínii* . . . that is
. . . eh . . . I presented a petition . . . eh. . . ."

" I know," said the secretary.

" The bishop said . . . it was
too soon. . . ."

" I know," repeated the host,
keeping his motionless eyes fixed
on Father Anton all the while.

" I have six little children . . .
and I . . . have been working
the school . . . and as for the
rubric . . ."

" I know," muttered the secretary again. Father Anton heaved
a deep sigh. This motionless
gaze fixed on him seemed almost
to paralyse him, and he felt that
he should never find courage to
put his hand in his pocket and

draw out the letter on which everything depended.

"I have now come to place myself in your hands. . . . All my hopes depend upon you," continued he, and suddenly he felt for his pocket with his hand, but his fingers after fumbling about a little, returned to their former position on his knee.

"But supposing that the bishop . . ." began the secretary, but he was here interrupted by Father Anton.

"I have prepared a petition which I venture to hand you."

"A petition? . . . Well, that may be useful."

The deacon hastily drew the envelope out of his pocket and was horrified at its crumpled untidy appearance.

"I fear . . . the envelope is crumpled!" said he, convulsively clutching it with his trembling fingers. The step he was about to take would either make or mar him. And supposing that Father Pankrátii and the *blago-*

tshínii were only making fun of
him when they told him those
stories.

"Very well, your petition shall
receive due attention," said the
secretary, fixing his eyes on the
letter.

The deacon placed the letter
on the edge of the writing-table,
and forthwith got up and bowed.
The secretary took the envelope
in a careless manner and moved
it to the centre of the table.
Father Anton was already in the
entrance hall. He had never
been in such a hurry as he was
on this occasion. He pictured
to himself the probable result of
his action. The secretary, most
likely, having opened the envelope
and found the bank note, had
turned pale, and was trembling
with anger and would rush
after him, crying, " How dare
you ! I ! The secretary ! You !
Deacon ? Eh ? The bishop will
inform the synod ! You shall
be unfrocked, and sent to the
monastery to do penance ! "

"Oh Lord, save and help me!" exclaimed the deacon mentally, thrusting his left foot in his golosh. "What have I done? What have I done? Ruined my wife and family!"

Some such scene appeared to him inevitable : the secretary would be sure to take offence. To offer so highly placed a personage a bribe! It was dreadful! And what should he want money for with his large salary?

The deacon hastily descended the staircase and gained the street, but still no one pursued him. Once in the open air he became calmer, and even decided to wait there a minute or two. If he was to perish, it was better to know the worst at once. Why linger in suspense? He looked anxiously up the staircase leading to the secretary's apartments ; everything was silent and motionless as before.

At length, having thoroughly regained his self-possession, he

saw that it was extremely un-
likely that he would be pursued,
and felt convinced that the con-
tents of his letter would appeal
most eloquently to the secretary's
heart ; in fact, that the thing was
now settled.

Having thus consoled himself,
he resolved to keep away as far
as possible from the consistorium
and the bishop's palace for the
rest of the day.   In an unlucky
moment he might fall under his
lordship's eye and thus spoil
everything.   But the whole of
the day was still before him and
had to be got through somehow.

He lingered for some time
about the market place where he
met several of his parishioners,
and then returning to the inn
tried to sleep, but his mental
agitation was too great.

He had a good many friends
among the lesser clergy in the
town, but he resolved to keep
clear of them all.   Questions
would doubtless be asked as to

the object of his visit, and he would most likely be unable to restrain himself, and would say that he had come to present a petition that he should be promoted to the priesthood, and this would give rise to endless jokes, jealousies, and other unpleasantnesses. It was better not to disturb the even tenour of their lives. It was the excitement of anticipation that kept him awake ; he had little fear as to the ultimate issue. The secretary was a man of high influence, and having accepted the bribe there was little doubt that he would use his influence.

Nevertheless, Father Anton thought it wise to visit the *blagotshínii.* He did not intend to ask any favour of the dignitary, but merely to pay his respects.

The *blagotshínii* was well disposed towards him, and had put in a good word for him to the bishop, so he felt bound to show his gratitude for this.

The *blagotshínii* lived in a
smart little house, and everything in the interior looked
bright and inviting—the polished
wooden staircase, the little glass
conservatory filled with plants,
and the small, snug, bright
rooms with their comfortable
furniture decorated with blue
and pink satin, the charming
wife and merry children—the
whole surroundings, in fact, made
a pleasant impression on all who
visited the house.

It was easy to see that all
guests, whether highly placed or
humble, were received with equal
warmth.

" Ah, Anton, so' you've come !
Very glad to see you ! Come in
here, Anióuta," said he, calling
his wife. " Father Anton has
come—you know, from Boutistchévka ! Have tea brought in.
You will have some tea, Father
Anton, and some jam ? And tell
me, how is your wife's health ?
And Father Pankrátii ? Always
busy with his affairs, I suppose ?

Here comes my eldest daughter;
don't be afraid, Nióura, come
and speak to Father Anton; he
does not bite. . . ."

The *matóushka* and other
children made their appearance,
and tea was served, and Father
Anton's hosts made him feel
quite at home. Father Iohann,
the *blagotshínii*, lived quite in
the style of a layman. Nothing
in his home surroundings reminded one of his sacred calling,
or that he held a post which is
looked upon as the high road to
the dignity of protopope. His
study walls were not adorned
with the usual view of Mount
Athos or amateur sketches; but
there were several geographical
maps and a solitary landscape
in a black frame. A bookcase
with glass doors contained
handsomely bound volumes with
such names as the following
printed on their backs: " Schlos-
·ser," " Buckle," " Schiller,"
" Poushkine," " Tourgenieff,"
&c.,—names whose significance

failed to impress Father Anton.
A pianoforte stood in the drawing-
room ; the *matóushka* played a
valse on it and the children
danced.

Father Anton was invited to
stay for dinner. He had not yet
succeeded in getting a private
talk with the *blagotshínii*, and
was longing to tell him about
his visit to the secretary that
morning ; and was burning to
confide the story of his success
to some one. Such an occasion
offered itself after dinner. He
was sitting with his host in the
study. The *blagotshínii* was
luxuriously reclining on a soft
sofa smoking a cigar. The deacon
had been offered a cigar, but
declined ; he was unaccustomed
to this form of tobacco, and used
generally to smoke very thick
cigarettes of his own manufacture,
using a piece of reed grown in his
own parish as a mouthpiece.

" I have seen the secretary .
to-day, Father *blagotshínii !* "
remarked the deacon.

" Aha, about that business of yours, I suppose. . . ."

" Yes . . . I asked him to help me, and he promised to do what he could. . . . He is a stern man. . . . Very conscientious in the performance of his duties, I should think."

" I don't know; I have nothing to do with the consistorium. The bishop wanted me to become a member, but I refused. All sorts of intrigues go on there ! "

" Do you know, Father *blagotshínii*, that I left a letter with him . . . with a petition, he! he! he ! . . ." continued Anton, in a lower tone, looking anxiously at the door.

" It's a very strange thing, but if I don't smoke a cigar after dinner, I feel just as if I had not dined at all," remarked the *blagotshínii*.

" Habit, I suppose," rejoined the guest, thinking to himself uneasily—" I begin about the letter and he turns off the subject to cigars."

Strains of music were heard in the adjoining room. Father Anton continued—

" I handed him my letter, and he put it down on the middle of the table and said, ' That will do.' . . ."

" Play us something of Mendelssohn's, Anióuta," exclaimed the dignitary, calling out to his wife; and turning round to his guest, said—" I am very fond of Mendelssohn. He is my favourite composer—listen! . . . *Romance sans paroles.*"

The deacon had to listen, and the conversation did not again turn upon the secretary and the letter.

He returned at dusk to the inn through the streets, which were already lit up. His thoughts turned on the pleasant news awaiting him on the morrow at the consistorium. What fine results his expedition was to bring him! and he pictured Natiónka's and Douniásha's delight when he returned to them a priest. He also thought, what strange characters one meets with in life ! The secretary, for instance, if one could believe all that was said of him, was the possessor of a house worth 200,000 roubles, and yet he would take one hundred roubles from a poor man ! And then the *blagotshinii*, who would not even listen to his story ! He either did not care to hear it, or perhaps did not wish to mix himself up in these matters. And then, what a contrast there was between these two men ! The one, gloomy repellent, and the other, pleasant, cheerful, and everything about him bright ! They both held lucrative posts and lived in good style, each in their own way.

To be deacon in a poor parish with six children and an invalid wife was sad contrast to all this.

The next morning, at twelve o'clock, Anton was walking in the bishop's garden on the evenly-rolled gravel paths. He knew

that this was the hour when the
secretary was received in audience by his reverence, and was
anxiously awaiting the issue.
He mentally depicted the scene
which was being enacted. The
secretary unfolds his petition
and reads it: "Ah," says the
bishop, "that is the fellow who
cannot sing in tune! I have
already told him that he must
wait!"—"Your reverence," re-
plies the secretary, "that was
merely an accidental circumstance, and occurred because he
was not given a chance of practis-
ing it up, but he is really a
worthy and capable man; he
has six children, and I take this
opportunity of mentioning his
name to your reverence. . . ."
Anton pictured to himself the
secretary's long speech, which
the bishop listens to with attention, and is finally persuaded to
grant the petition. The bishop
then says, "Well, I see there is
nothing else to be done! You
have convinced me, secretary!

Give me the pen!" and forthwith the prelate takes the pen
and writes—"I am well pleased
to lay hands on the deacon Anton
Boubuirko, and will raise him to
the dignity of priesthood." The
secretary folds up this document,
and, placing it in his portfolio,
returns to the consistorium. One
o'clock has struck. He must
give the secretary time to hand
the document to the clerk. He
knows this clerk—he is a very,
very old man, who has served in
the consistorium almost since
its first inauguration. He is
clean shaven like the secretary,
but not so big, and, unlike him,
he is bald, and of a jovial disposition. In times gone by, when
there was a secretary who wore
whiskers, he also wore whiskers.
He would very likely have to
give this man a trifle also.

Two o'clock struck. Anton
calculated that all formalities
must be completed by this time,
and started off to the consistorium. He found the clerk en-

grossed in the work of comparing
the copy of some document with
its original.

" One minute, please, *bátioushka*," said he with a smile.
Being toothless, his smile was
not an agreeable one. Father
Anton waited, feeling perfectly
calm, and had no unpleasant
apprehension as to the verdict
awaiting him.

" The deacon Anton Bou-
buirko ?," asked the clerk. " Let
me see—yes, here is your petition ! "

He took up the petition from
the table and put it right up to
Anton's nose. The deacon read
the bishop's remark written under
it in blue pencil : " This petition
is untimely, the petitioner has not
learned to sing in tune." Lower
down on the paper was written
in black ink, in the secretary's
hand—" Refusal."

" That is all, I think," added
the clerk, again smiling, and
placing the letter back on the
table.

Father Anton's head seemed
all in a whirl at that moment.
A mist rose before his eyes and
obscured from him the head clerk
and his assistants and another
deacon who had entered, and was
bowing low and making some
request with tears in his eyes.
What had happened ? Natiónka
was crying. Douniásha was
looking as black as thunder, a
thing he had never before seen.
Mariána Pankratiévna was demanding her money back and
repeating, " I am very sorry for
you, father deacon; my terms are
hard, I know ; " and the *blagotshínii*, jolly-looking as ever,
was standing somewhere high up
in the clouds smoking a cigar
and laughing. But this vision
only lasted a minute. Father
Anton suddenly recollected and
thought, " I have given him too
little ! " and then a daring project
arose in his mind—to go to the
secretary, and, in the presence of
all the officials, members of the
consistorium, and petitioners,

ask him, " How much more do you want, Mr. Secretary ? " But then from bold projects, conceived, in the mind of a country deacon, to bold actions is a very long way. So he did not go to the secretary after all, but returned to the inn. He ordered his conveyance, harnessed his horse, and paid his reckoning with the innkeeper almost mechanically. He was even surprised that his feelings, especially with regard to Natiónka and the children, did not overwhelm him. But such despair as his was not of the ordinary kind. He was too much stunned to let his grief overcome him. It was only late that night, when still ten versts from home, that he suddenly started up and beat his horse pitilessly. Some unknown cause urged him to push on home as fast as possible.

Arriving back about midnight, he was surprised to see lights in his windows at so late an hour.

Natiónka was prostrated with
a bad attack of fever, and was in
a delirious state. The deacon
was met by his sister with tears
in her eyes. The children were
asleep in another room, with the
exception of the eldest one, Marínka, who was sitting on the
foot of the bed looking at her
mother with a terrified expression.

"What is the matter with
her?" asked Father Anton.

"Sh-h! . . . come in here."

Douniásha took hold of the
sleeve of his cassock and pulled
him into the kitchen. She then
sat down, flung her arms on the
table, and buried her head in her
hands and burst out crying.

"Anton, Anton, how unlucky
you are!" she exclaimed.

"Yes, unlucky in every respect!" whispered Father Anton.

The presentiment of that which
he was about to be told so over-
came him that he dared not ask
any further questions.

"Almost immediately after you

had started she went to bed,"
said Douniásha, trying to restrain
her tears. "Her head was splitting, and her chest was stifled
as though weighed down with a
rock, and she was seized with
such a terrible fit of coughing
that hemorrhage set in. . . . We
got frightened, and sent for the
village surgeon. . . . He came
and examined her, and, taking
me aside, said, 'You know the
matóushka has got consumption
in its very worst form . . . I
fear she can scarcely live more
than a few days longer.'"

The deacon's knees trembled,
and he involuntarily sank down
on a chair. He was as pale as
a ghost, but did not weep, only
his lower lip trembled convulsively, and his eyes, immovably
fixed on Douniásha, frightened
the latter by their senseless expression.

"And do you know," muttered
he, in a feeble childlike voice,
"my journey, too, has been in
vain. . . . I gave the secretary a

hundred roubles, which I bor-
rowed from Mariána, but it was
all in vain, because I can't sing
. . . in tu-u-une!"

Anton was here overcome with
floods of tears. His sister approached him and tried to console him by saying that the
surgeon knew nothing about it;
but all her efforts were in vain,
for Anton continued to sob like a
woman, hitting his head pitilessly
against the table.

"You will disturb her," said
Douniásha. He then got up and
began to walk about on the earth
floor of the kitchen with both his
hands up to his face.

"Douniásha, Douniásha, what
is to become of us? . . . Lord,
have mercy!" . . . muttered he,
casting a glance at the *eikon*
in the corner, blackened with
smoke, as though he there expected to find a way out of all his
troubles. Douniásha leant her
head against the cold wall and
wept silently.

The door opened and Mária

entered. Mária, usually gay and
careless, was now pale and her
eyelids swollen.

"The *matóushka* wants to see
you! . . ."

"Me?" . . . asked Anton, and
taking off his mud-stained cassock,
began to wash his face, and
especially his eyes, in order to
remove all traces of his tears,
and, after combing his hair, went
quietly on tip-toes to the next
room. He exerted the whole of
his small stock of self-possession
to keep his voice and face calm,
and even to look happy.

"Why, Natiónka! What is
the matter with you? Good Lord!
You have taken to your bed! . . ."
said he, in a quiet voice, kissing
her burning forehead.

"Yes, Anton, and I am going
to take to my grave ; God is
punishing us for our sins." She
was here attacked by a most
distressing fit of coughing.

"What are you talking about,
Natiónka? You will get better
again! When the sun gets a

little bit warm you will get up
again. . . ."

But Anton felt that the tone
of his voice belied his words.
Worst of all, he was suddenly
attacked by a fit of stammering,
which at ordinary times he was
free from, and this betrayed his
real anxiety.

"The sun will get warm again
but I shall never feel it," said
Natiónka, slowly shaking her
head. "But if only it will warm
my children! I feel that my
end is near. . . . The surgeon
knows it, and Douniásha's tears,
and I heard you just now in the
kitchen. . . . I feel it, Anton—I
feel it! I wish to talk to you a
little. . . . But first take Marínka up to bed; she should not
be here."

"Come along, Marinotshka, to
bed!" said Father Anton, turning round to the little girl.

But Marínka clutched her
mother's feet convulsively with
both her little arms.

"No; I don't wish to leave

mamma! I will never leave her.
. . . I will go into the grave
with her!" exclaimed the child.

Natiónka's eyes became moist.

"Let her stay," whispered the
mother; "sit down, Anton—take
a chair and sit down." Anton
obeyed.

"Tell me, how did you get on in
the town? Has the bishop consented?"

"The bishop . . . nothing
special! . . . Nothing, Natiónka!"

"Do not deceive me, Anton!
I may not be alive to-morrow.
Tell me the truth. Has he
refused?"

"He has, Natiónka," muttered
Anton, in a low voice, letting his
head fall on his breast.

"Altogether or only tempo-
rarily?"

"For a time, Natiónka! He
wrote, 'The petition is ill-timed,
as he cannot sing in tune.' In
tune—the Lord help us!"

"Is this the truth, Anton?"

"It is, Natiónka, I swear it!"

"And how are you to educate
our six children? And, Anton,"
added she in a lower tone of
voice, so that Marínka should
not overhear, but the little girl
pricked up her ears and did not
lose a single word; "if I die
you will be left a widower."

"Good Lord!" whispered Anton.

"You will be a widower, Anton . . . and widowers are never
made priests. . . . It is illegal.
. . . Exception is only made in
special cases, when the widower
is over forty. But you, Anton,
have never done anything to
deserve such an exception being
made in your favour."

Anton got up, sighed, put his
hand to his forehead, and sat
down again.

"Oh, Lord, Lord!" he whispered, and raising his hand made
the sign of the cross.

"This is no time for indeci-
sion, Anton; you must consider
the best thing to be done! . . .
Remember the six! If you re-

main a deacon for life, surrounded
by such poverty as we now live
in, our children will be beggars.
And what have they done, poor
things, to deserve such a
fate ? "

" What is to be done ?—it is
the Lord's will ! "

" If I die, you remain a deacon
for life."

" I cannot think of any way
out of our trouble, Natiónka."

Father Anton was indeed too
much overwhelmed by misfortune
to be in a state to view the situation calmly. He seemed to have
lost all power of thinking, and it
only remained for him to bow
silently to his fate. His feelings
were further harassed by his
wife's terrible cough.

" Listen, Anton; lose no time
. . . you are not a widower so
long as I am alive. . . . Go off
at once to the bishop. . . . Do
not lose a minute. . . . Entreat
him on your knees, tell him everything. . . . Tell him that I am
dying, and that your last chance

will be gone. The bishop will
take pity on you. . . . Go."

She was again seized with a
fit of coughing, after which she
added in a breathless voice—

"Go! . . . fall at his feet . . .
for I shall die to-morrow, and
you will be a deacon for ever."

"Natiónka, Natiónka, what
are you saying? . . . Heaven have
mercy on us both!"

"I say—go! . . . Go, Anton!
. . . Remember the children. . . .
Go!"

"How can I go if you are . . .
how can I, Natiónka?"

"I can die without you, if God
so wills. Go at once!"

"Natiónka, I cannot—I cannot
leave you!"

"Anton, come nearer to me.
. . . Give me your hand. . . .
Like that! We have lived for
eight years together, and you
have always gratified my wishes.
. . . Are you going to refuse my
request now? . . . now that I am
dying? . . . I implore you, in the
name of all that is sacred, to go!

. . . Anton, my dear! It is my last request! Go. . . . I feel sure that the bishop's heart will be touched. . . . It will indeed! . . . See there, our dear sensible little girl, Marínka, is she to grow up without education? . . . and the others, too. . . . Kiss me, and start off to the town. . . . If God so wills, I shall await your return, and gladly shall I die, if all is fulfilled. . . . Now go, my dear Anton. . . ."

Father Anton, overcome with religious emotion of a nature which he had never before experienced, made the sign of the cross over her thrice in a slow and deliberate manner, and then kissed her lips. He then took Marínka in his arms, and also crossed her and kissed her, after which he went into the room where the other children were sleeping and repeated this action to each of them.

" I will go," he said in a hoarse but firm voice. " As it is your desire, and you feel . . . I will go! It is bitter for me . . . terribly bitter, but I will go as you order me, Natiónka."

His step became firmer, and his look more self-possessed. He was imbued with the idea that he was executing Natiónka's wish —perhaps her last wish.

Anton went out into the vestibule, and from thence into the yard. The stars were still twinkling faintly, and the first pale light of early dawn was lighting up the sky. Father Anton went into the shed where his horse stood. This miserable beast looked utterly exhausted and dejected after its long journey. Father Anton saw that his horse could not possibly carry him another forty versts in its present condition, besides which, he had no time to lose. To-day was Saturday. If the bishop would take pity on him the ceremony must either be performed on the following day, otherwise a week must elapse till the next Sunday, and who could say what a week

would bring forth. He returned
again to the yard.

" Mária," said he, " run immediately to the post station and
order a pair of horses and a
dilijan . . . I am going back
again to the town. And tell
them not to put a bell on."

" To the town ? " asked Douniásha.

" Yes, Douniásha, I am sent
by my wife."

" For the doctor ? "

" Ah, Douniásha, I fear the
doctor can do but little good
now . . . The village surgeon
was right. She has so far re-
lapsed in a single day that death
must now be imminent. She
knows it herself ! . . . "

" Then why are you going to
the town ? "

" On business which I myself
hardly understand, Douniásha.
It is better to ask no questions
about it . . . Perhaps Natiónka
will tell you . . . I go at her
request . . . I rely entirely on
you, Douniásha . . . Take care of

her . . . and in case of anything, which the Lord forbid . . . I shall return to-morrow. Alas! alas!"

He walked up and down the yard, looked in at the shed again and went down to the river. The postmaster delayed, and it was already broad daylight when a pair-horse conveyance drove up to the deacon's hut.

Father Anton hastily entered the house, bowed three times before the eikon, knelt down, whispered a prayer, and then turning to Natiónka said—

"I am starting, Natiónka. May your wish be fulfilled!" She only nodded her head encouragingly. He bent down his head and Natiónka placed her cold emaciated arms round his neck, and drawing his face near her cheek whispered—

"Good-bye, Anton! I will keep alive till you return; I have sufficient strength for that!"

He went out with uneven steps, and seated himself in the conveyance, which started off over the uneven and muddy road.

A journey of forty versts for a man with his soul weighed down by such griefs, doubts, and difficulties, seems an endless one.

Had he been alone he could have freely given vent to his feelings. But in front of him was seated the *yemstchik* Makár, one of the village peasants, who knew Father Anton well. Makár was curious to learn the cause of this sudden expedition.

" It's some important affair, I suppose, father deacon, which calls you so suddenly to the town. You always used to go with your own horse, and now, suddenly, you order post-horses. . . ."

" Because it is necessary," answered Anton.

" Some business affair, I suppose ? Has the bishop sent for you ? " asked Makár.

" Be silent, for God's sake! . . . Why do you bother me ? It is not your business. . . ."

Makár turned his back to the

deacon and was silent. The deacon's mind was occupied with subjects foreign to Makár and his questions. Impressions produced by events in times long since gone by, speculations concerning the misty, uncertain future, and thoughts about his wife laying on her bed of sickness, in turn presented themselves to his mind. The whole of his past life came back to him, and he pondered over it with feeling and deliberation, as though preparing himself for confession on some occasion of special solemnity.

He remembered his father, a village deacon with a large family. Up to the age of ten years old he had been allowed to run about with his brothers and sisters in the mud and the sun with bare feet ; no one looked after them, they could do what they liked ; and they saw many things with the observant eye of children, and found out things which other children should not, and do not, know. They were taught the alphabet by their father; he was an old man and taught them in the old style: the alphabet, the prayer book, and the psalms as the highest wisdom, and this was all. They first read the psalms, then learned them by heart — the old man could not devise any course of learning beyond this, for that was all he knew himself, excepting what was necessary in his clerical duties. At the age of ten he was suddenly taken off to the town and put to school.

This was one of the regular ante-reform schools, which Anton entered just before the abolition of the old system of instruction; but, notwithstanding the impending changes, it was still directed on the old lines. He was suddenly set down to learn Latin and Greek with the assistance of various instruments of torture, which exercised a terrible influence on this boy, who had always been accustomed to the freedom of life in the open air.

He understood nothing—neither the school discipline, nor the rules of Latin grammar—and he therefore used to be flogged, have his ears boxed, be shut up in a dark room—in fact, he was "taught," in the fullest sense of the word, according to former ideas of education. The recollection of this period in Anton's career only brings a feeling of wild pain at the stupid, senseless treatment he then received. Why should he have been thus treated? Every one ill-treated him from the head-master down to the most hopeless idler who could double his fists. But this state of things only lasted two years. Suddenly everything was radically changed.[1] All became polite and considerate towards him : new masters were appointed, who addressed him in the second person plural, rods and rulers were abolished, and

---

[1] These reforms were introduced during the reign of Alexander II.

no one was beaten, no one cried. But Anton was already crushed and frightened ; he made but slow progress with his learning, remained two years in each class, and earned for himself the nickname of "ass." He somehow managed to get into the seminary, remained there a year, but could not make any progress.

When Anton reached his twentieth year his old father, the deacon, was still alive, and began to think about a career in life for his son. The only opening that offered itself seemed to be the Church ; he was ordained sub-deacon, and it was probable that he would never attain a higher rank than that of deacon. There were many others whose prospects of further success than this were doubtful. But Anton was fortunate in one respect. It seems that not so very long ago a certain proto-presbyter died, a man of some importance in the diocese, who had formerly been *blagotshínii*,

and a member of the consistorium. This dignitary left a
very considerable fortune, and
directed in his will that a portion
of his money should be applied
to the foundation of a home for
orphan girls of the families of
the clergy. These girls were to
be educated and to be taught
needlework and housekeeping—
in fact, to be so brought up as
to make suitable wives for the
lesser clergy. Owing to the fact
that the founder had been held
in universal esteem, education
in this home conferred special
privileges on those who had
been its inmates. It soon became known that any one
choosing a wife from among the
girls educated there, acquired
the right of early promotion to
the rank of deacon. Anton was
one of those who benefited by
this privilege. At times, when
Anton was confidentially disposed, he would give his version
of the story such as the following:

" Bat'ka [1] says to me : ' Now,
my little son : you have finished
your education and been through
the course, and I see that you
don't want to be more learned
than your father was. Go and
choose a wife from the home
and then you will be a deacon,
anyhow. The deacon's bread,
God knows, is not very white,
but still it is whiter than the
sub-deacon's.' Well, what did
I care ? It was all the same
to me. I had not learned sense
then. I was quite ready to
marry ; of course, I understood
about the advantages of a wife.
. . . Well, I was sent off to
the home, together with my
parents and my father's brother-
in-law, also a deacon. On
arriving, we were taken straight
into the class-room. Of course,
all the girls knew that a suitor
was being brought to see them,
and they were all got up in their
best clothes, and were sitting

---

[1] Father—diminutive.

in a row, eight of them, some sewing, and some doing embroidery. . . . We entered, I, of course, keeping behind my relations; for, you know, I felt just a bit awkward . . . . An unknown man arrives and has to choose his companion for life forthwith. I was not quite so tall as I am now. We walked twice across the room and I had a look at all their faces. . . . Well, you know, it seemed rather like looking at goods in a shop or bazaar. However, it was no use walking about the room without doing anything. I had to make up my mind somehow. My mother came up to me and said, 'I should advise you, Antosha, to take that one over there with the light hair, doing the embroidery.' It so happened that I did not care for the light-haired girl, I cannot give any reason, but I did not fancy her. But near the corner I saw a dark girl, thin and pale; I looked at her and felt such pity for her,

for she looked so pinched, and
my heart beat faster. . . . There,
thought I, is my destiny! And
I said to my mother, ' No, I
don't care for the light one, I
prefer the dark-haired one over
there ! ' and pointed at her with
my finger. And mother replied,
' Well, it's your affair; I shall
not have to live with her.' After
this we left the room, and went
into Father Isidore's room for
refreshments. Father Isidore
was the director of the home.
I saw that my dark-haired girl
was already here, pouring out
tea : she turned red and I could
see that she was agitated. We
were introduced to each other,
and I learned that her name was
Nathália Parfentiévna, and I
straightway rechristened her
Natiónka in my mind. As soon
as we had drunk tea I discovered
that the others had disappeared
and left us two together. She
was seated on the sofa looking
out of the window, as though not
thinking about me at all. I saw

at once that they had purposely
left us together in order that I
should explain myself. I had
never before found myself alone
with a young girl, and had not
the least idea of how to set
about explaining my intentions
to her. My heart beat fast, as
I suppose it ought to have. I
became confused. Well, there
was nothing for it. I had to
make a beginning. I had come
to find a wife and had to find
one. So I went up to her and
said, ' Nathália Parfentiévna,
you must know what I am here
for very well, so it is not necessary to explain. I wish to have
you as my wife and to become
a deacon; the most reverend
bishop has promised to lay his
hands on me, and has even found
a place for me at the village of
Boutistchévka, although there is
no regular deacon's place there.'
Her eyes dropped—' I know all
. . . I agree ! '—And then I
even kissed her hand. The
following day we were mar-

ried, and I was ordained
deacon."

This was Anton's version of
the story when in a happy frame
of mind ; but, of course, under the
present circumstances, the details
of this history presented themselves to him under a different
aspect. This episode all came
back to him with tenderness, but
his spirit was laden with grief.
He and Natiónka had got on well
together—indeed, they seemed
to have been created one for the
other. Children came to them
one after another " without any
interval," as Natiónka used to
express it, and their poverty
increased with each fresh arrival.
Natiónka's health had from the
first been feeble, but she had
always kept on her feet, and
only during the last two years
had showed signs of giving in.
Father Anton had been a model
churchman, and the bishop was
well disposed towards him, and
there was every probability that
he would be raised to the

priestly dignity ere long. The
fact of Natiónka coming from
the home was all in his favour.
Then came that unfortunate in-
cident about his failure to sing
in tune, and the flame of hope
expired with a flash. The recollection of happy days spent
with Natiónka came back to
Anton's memory, when he was
at length counting on obtaining
a living, and that Natiónka would
recover her health, and all would
be well with them. And suddenly such an unlooked-for, im-
probable misfortune !

· He was now going to town at
his wife's urgent request. Maybe
the bishop would have pity on
him and grant his petition. But,
if Natiónka was not to share his
good fortune, what joy would
there be ? And how could he
live without Natiónka ? He was
only twenty-eight years old. Life
was still before him. The future
appeared to him like a cold, dark
tomb. . . .

When he thought of that which

was passing at home, his heart
bled, and a cold chill ran over his
body. Natiónka was lying there
on her deathbed, and he was on
his way to town to petition for
promotion. It seemed a dreadful
thing to be thinking about promotion at a moment when the
person nearest his heart was
dying ! . . .

But then the six children ?—
the loss of a single minute might
perhaps render him a widower,
and consequently a pauper for
life, and his children—beggars.

At length the town was reached.
Again he drove through the
muddy streets of that town from
which, only yesterday, he had
been so relentlessly and unfairly
driven. A second time he entered
it as a humble petitioner, but this
time feelings of quite a different
nature had possession of him.
Father Anton pulled out his
watch and looked at the time.
It was nearly mid-day. Just the
time when the bishop received
visitors in audience.

" Go straight to the bishop's palace, as quick as you can! " he cried to Makár.

Makár urged on his horses, and they plunged forward, scattering the liquid mud in all directions with their feet. On reaching the entrance to the palace, Anton got down. Makár said to him—

" Eh, father deacon, you can't go into the bishop's palace all covered with mud? . . . Your cassock and face and hair are all bespattered with it."

Father Anton paid no attention to this remark. He only drew his sleeve across his forehead, thus smearing the mud over his face, and ran up to the private door leading to the bishop's rooms.

III.

THERE were about ten people waiting in the spacious reception room of the bishop, which was furnished with rows of uncomfortable looking chairs placed against the walls, adorned with portraits of metropolitans and other important personages in the clerical world. The majority of those seeking an audience with the bishop belonged to various ranks of the clergy; they were all carefully got up for the occasion with their hair oiled and combed, and were standing in the centre of the reception room. The bishop had not yet made his appearance, but was expected every minute.

A young monk with rosy cheeks had looked into the room several times in order to count the number of the visitors. The bishop was engaged with some person of greater importance than the others, who had been admitted into the inner room. The petitioners had long since worked up the expressions of their faces to the highest pitch of calm devoutness, when a strange conversation was heard going on in the outer hall, in tones, perhaps, never before heard in these stately precincts, where people usually walk on tip-toes and converse in whispers.

"Excuse me, *bátioushka*, but I can't let you in like this! I must first ask the lay brother," said the hall porter.

"I don't care, I wish to see the bishop—the bishop himself," replied a tenor voice, stuttering with excitement.

" But you must wipe your feet, *bátioushka*, and clean yourself up a bit. . . . You can't go in as

you are. . . . You will cover
the floors with mud ! " exclaimed
the porter.

" No, no, it does not matter. . . . I cannot stop to think
about that ! "

To judge from the sounds that
were then heard it seemed as if
resistance was being made to the
entry of the new-comer.

" I can't let you in, *bátioushka!*"

" Get away ! "

" Very well ; it will be the
worse for you ! "

" I don't care ! It cannot be
worse. Let me pass ! "

" As you like."

Looks of astonishment now
replaced the former pious expressions of the visitors waiting in
the reception room. Father
Anton rushed into the room,
past the porter, with clods of
mud on his huge boots, his
face unwashed, and his hair dishevelled—

" Has his reverence come out
yet ? " exclaimed Father Anton,

in a tone of voice quite out of
keeping with the solemn surroundings.

"No, he has not," replied the
others, looking with astonishment
at the petitioner who dared to
present himself in such an unceremonious manner.

The lay brother, hearing the
disturbance, came out from the
inner room, and seeing Father
Anton, went up to him.

"What do you mean, *bátioushka*, by coming here in such a
manner?"

Father Anton gazed down at
this little man with an air of
profound contempt.

"Get away, for God's sake!"
exclaimed he, with such tone and
emphasis that the lay brother
moved off quickly, almost pre-
cipitately, and shrugged his
shoulders. At this moment
Father Iohann, the *blagotshínii*,
came out from the inner room with
a bundle of papers in his hands.
He had just been having an
interview with the bishop.

Seeing Father Anton, he approached him—

" What does this mean, father deacon ? "

" I am determined to present myself to his reverence, Father *blagotshínii*."

" You are ruining your prospects for life."

" Ah, Father *blagotshínii*, things cannot be worse with me than they are now," muttered Father Anton.

" The *blagotshínii* took him aside and whispered—

" I hope you are not going to compromise any one."

Father Anton at once grasped his meaning. The *blagotshínii* evidently thought that he had come to complain of the secretary for taking a bribe.

" Ah, it is not that, that I have come here about—it is not that, Father *blagotshínii*. I am in such trouble ! " said he, clenching his fist against his breast.

" What about ? "

At this moment the bishop

himself entered the room. He
was a tall, vigorous looking old
man, and was clad in a dark blue
silk cassock; he wore a long
silky grey beard; the expression
of his countenance was severe,
and inspired the respect of all.
When receiving visitors in
audience he scarcely ever spoke,
but only listened and observed.
He possessed a most remarkable
memory, used to remember all
he had heard, and afterwards
form his decisions in his study.

"Who is making all this noise
here?" asked his lordship, but
instead of receiving an answer,
he heard the sound of hurried
steps across the room, and some
one threw himself down at his
feet, clutching him by the knees.

"Please, your reverence, it is
I. . . . It is my great grief that
makes me noisy."

The bishop's first impulse
was to get away from this
impetuous supplicant. His face
reddened with anger; but when
he saw that the mud-stained

individual before him was none
other than deacon Anton Bou-
buírko, when he heard his
trembling voice and his stammering, disjointed speech, his
heart softened, and he said—

"What is your trouble about?
Get up, deacon!"

"Unheard of trouble! My
wife . . . your reverence, is
dying. . . . Oh, Lord God! . . .
she is dying . . . she is dying,
your reverence!"

It was impossible to catch the
meaning of Father Anton's words
after this, for his voice became
choked with sobbing.

The bishop was in perplexity
as to what to do with this man,
but then seeing that he could get
no coherent statement from him,
said to Father Iohann—

"Father *blagotshínii* try and
find out what he wants me to do
for him."

"Come along with me, father
deacon," said the *blagotshínii*,
catching hold of him by the
sleeve of his cassock.

Father Anton got up and
quietly followed the *blagotshínii.* They passed through
a low door into a small room,
fitted up with a marble wash-
hand-stand and a looking-glass,
and the *blagotshínii,* shaking
his head, said—

" How can you act thus, father
deacon ? It is not hard to en-
rage the bishop."

" I know not what I am doing,
Father *blagotshínii.* . . . I am
overcome with trouble. Natiónka, my wife, is dying of consumption . . . Oh, Lord my God ! if
not to-day, then to-morrow, I
shall become a widower, and all
will be over with me. . . . A
deacon for life, Father *blagotshínii* . . . and what shall I do
with my six children ? My wife,
poor thing, sent me here ; she is
dying, but still she made me go.
' Think of the children,' she said.
. . . ' I will die without you . . .
and perhaps the bishop may
have pity on you.' . . . Just
think of my position, Father

blagotshínii! . . . My wife dying, and I am here . . . perhaps she is already dead, and then . . . father *blagotshínii!*

Suddenly, to the *blagotshínii's* astonishment, the deacon fell on his knees and stretched out his arms to him in supplication. Father Iohann endeavoured to calm and console him.

"In a few minutes the bishop will have finished his audience, and we will tell him all about it! You wait quietly and I will explain it to him."

"Very well, Father *blagotshínii*," said Anton, in a firmer voice, seating himself on a chair with a high back. Twenty minutes elapsed, during which time the deacon was unable to collect his thoughts.

The audience ended, Father Iohann explained Anton's position as best he could to the bishop.

The latter ordered Father Anton to be sent for.

On re-entering the audience

chamber, Anton saw there was no one there excepting the bishop, Father Iohann, and the lay brother. When he found himself face to face with the bishop he trembled.

" Supposing your wife is dead, you are already a widower," said the bishop.

" God's will be done," humbly replied Anton.

" And you ask to be made a priest, knowing very well that priesthood is not conferred on widowers under forty years of age ? "

" I know it, your reverence."

" How can I grant your request ? This would have to be answered for before God."

" Your reverence ! We shall answer ! My six little children entreat you ! . . . "

The bishop was silent and walked up and down the room several times.

"Your wife may still be alive!" said he at length, half to himself. " I am really sorry for you. . .

You are a worthy man. Six
children, you say—six? All
young, eh? H'm. . . . How
comes it that you have produced
children so recklessly? Well,
deacon, we will take the respon-
sibility on ourselves for the sake
of the children. Prepare yourself for the morrow!"

"Your reverence!" exclaimed
Father Anton. He wished to
stretch out his hand, but at that
moment his head became giddy
and his strength failed him. The
bishop and the lay brother supported him.

"Ah, poor fellow!" said the
bishop, feelingly, and shook his
head. "He must be encouraged.
As regards his wife, who knows,
God may lengthen her days; but
if not . . . In all things, His
will be done!" he added, addressing the *blagotshínii* and the
lay brother, and retired, deeply
affected, to his study. "Ah,
indeed, such is life and its difficulties!" thought the bishop,
walking up and down his study,

nervously fingering his rosary;
"and we sit quietly in our rooms
ignorant of it all, having absolute
power over all this grey mass of
humanity. All we know of their
lives is by reports and petitions,
and through the representations
of the consistorium. I have been
torturing this poor man because
he could not sing in tune: it was
merely a caprice of mine; and
all the while he has been suffering from such terrible misfortune
and assailed by such pressing
problems." At this moment the
bishop, moved to an outburst of
kindly feeling by the scene he
had just witnessed, experienced
a desire to see for himself how
the clergy under his control
really live, what hardships and
anxieties fall to the lot of these
humble deacons and sub-deacons,
weighed down by family troubles,
and ever dreaming of promotion.

Father Anton, on recovering
consciousness, slowly left the
episcopal palace. He was neither
in a state to rejoice or to

lament. His feeble mind could
not thoroughly realise all the
various emotions which he had
experienced in the course of the
last two or three days. Terror
at handing the secretary the
envelope, the bright ray of hope
which followed the acceptation
of the same, the *blagotshínii's*
hospitable reception, the disappointment which awaited him at
the consistorium, despair at his
wife's hopeless condition, the
struggle between the sentiments
of love for his wife and his duty
to his children, the scene in the
bishop's room, and the ceremony
to be performed on the morrow
—all these various experiences
had come upon him so abruptly
that his thoughts and feelings
were now, for the moment, para-
lysed. He was to endure a
terrible calamity, in the loss of
his wife, simultaneously with the
greatest piece of good fortune
that he could ever look for—the
attainment of the priestly dignity.
This indeed seemed almost a

supernatural coincidence of two diametrically opposed feelings. There is no greater calamity for a person in the clerical profession than the loss of his wife, especially if he loves her, as Anton loved Natiónka. Such a loss implies solitude for the rest of his days—singleness for evermore, surrounded by the world and its temptations, in a calling which demands absolute integrity of life. On the other hand, priesthood is the highest aspiration of such men as Anton, and therefore its attainment is the greatest good fortune which can befal them. Both these ideas came simultaneously into the deacon's mind, and at this moment he felt guilty in his conduct towards Natiónka. In her dying moments she was unselfishly thinking only of the future happiness of her husband and children, and possibly enduring terrible suspense at this very instant, while he was thinking about his career, and preparing himself for promotion. Notwithstanding his efforts, Father Anton completely failed to reconcile these two conflicting emotions. Thus it was that for the rest of the day, and during the evening which he passed in church trying in vain to attend to the service, for he had to prepare himself for the ceremony of the next day, and all night as he lay awake, and even the following morning during the celebration of mass when his promotion was being accomplished, he remained in a state of dull indifference and insensibility. His heart ached intolerably, his face was pale and his eyes sunken. Even the bishop standing at the altar remarked his careworn face, and said to him in a low tone—

" Have courage, Anton; think not of earthly things ! Remember the office you are assuming ! "

But Father Anton could not take courage, and remained till the end of the mass in the same semi - conscious state. When the ceremony was over he approached the bishop and said, joining his hands together, and by this gesture requesting the bishop's blessing—

"Your reverence, bless me, and let me go home! God will repay you for your goodness!"

The tone with which he uttered these words expressed profound sorrow and blind resignation to fate.

"Go, Father Anton, go! Your case is a special one!" said the bishop, blessing him, making a large sign of the cross over him.

Father Anton hastily took off the priestly vestments which, had circumstances been different, he would have worn for the first time with feelings of heartfelt joy.

But he was in no mood for rejoicing now. He hastened from the church to the post-station, where he demanded the best horses they had, instantly, as he wished to perform the

9

journey without a single stop-
page. He neither saw, nor
listened to what the postmaster
and driver said, but seated himself in the dilijan and implored
the *yemstchik* to lose no time.
This *yemstchik* was a good
fellow, and Father Anton gladly
gave him two roubles *na vód-
kou.*[1] The horses galloped along
at full speed through the mud
and over the holes in the road.

The narrow bed of the stream
flowing through Boutistchévka at
length came in sight, and beyond
it the house occupied by the
new proprietor, Skridloff. Father
Anton tried in vain to distinguish
his hut, but he could not see it;
he felt that if only he could see
a little corner of it, he would
learn the whole truth. Thoughts
flashed through his mind one
after another. First he saw a
gloomy picture of death: Natiónka lying thin, yellow, and
cold; all the children with

---

[1] Drink money.

frightened looks silently hud-
dling themselves up in a corner
of the room, except Marínka, her
mother's favourite, who sadly
looked at Natiónka's dead body
with her silent, thoughtful, big
eyes; Douniásha was weeping,
her face anxiously turned
towards the window to see if
Anton was coming. The deacon's heart almost burst. A
minute later, all this seemed
absurd, impossible, and wild.
Why? Why so soon? Natiónka
might get better, and live for
many years to come. With what
feelings of joy would she learn
that he had returned home a
priest! He then felt sure that
this was so, and that it could
not be otherwise, and urged
the *yemstchik* to hurry on in
order to reassure Natiónka. If
only she was still living, joy
might help to cure her of her
illness! Now that he was a
priest he would certainly receive
an appointment as parish priest
somewhere; he would have

plenty to live upon, and would
educate the children.

They had now reached Skridloff's house, and were driving
past his garden and a row of
earth huts. Anton now beheld
his stack yard; and from behind
a straw stack he could see his
thatched roof. Douniásha is
running out to meet him. . . .
What news does she bring? He
cannot contain himself; his heart
will break.

Stop!

The horses were suddenly
brought to a standstill; he
jumped out of the dilijan. Douniásha let her head fall on his
breast and sobbed. . . .

" Natiónka? " asked he, in a
wild, imploring tone.

" She is no more, Antosha. . . .
She breathed her last in the
night! . . . After you had
started, she seemed better. . . .
I thought she was easier. . . .
But suddenly blood flowed . . .
we could not stop it . . . and it
suffocated her, poor thing! . . .

She mentioned you at the last.
. . . Her last words were—' May
God help him to attain the
priesthood ! ' "

" And He has indeed helped
me. . . . But nothing could help
her. . . . It is the Lord's holy
will ! " muttered Anton, wringing
his hands in despair, and looking
wildly at his sister.

He slowly entered his house
with the uneven gait of a man
who is utterly broken. When he
saw Natiónka lying on the table,
half-covered with a cloth, her
head surrounded with a wreath
of flowers, and four candles
placed near the pillow on which
her wan, wasted head rested, he
fell down before her and prayed
her silently to forgive him for
his want of attention to her, and
for having attained the priestly
rank too late to be able to share
with her its advantage.

There were about twenty
people in the room, chiefly consisting of peasant women, but
among others were Father Pan-

krátii's daughter and his housekeeper, Axinïa ; but when Father
Anton lifted his head he saw the
incumbent himself entering the
room, together with the clerk,
who was carrying the vestments
and the censer.

"Let us celebrate the re-
quiem!" said Father Anton, in
a solemn voice.

"Let us!" rejoined Father
Pankrátii, putting on his *riza.*[1]

The clerk handed Anton his
stichar,[2] but the latter shook his
head and said—

"No, get me a *riza.* . . . I
have this day been elevated to the
priesthood. . . . Ah, Natiónka,
all I can offer you are my
prayers!" exclaimed he in a
broken voice.

The children, with terrified
expressions on their faces, looked
in at the door, and Marínka
stood beside her mother gazing
earnestly, with her large melan-

[1] Chasuble, or cope worn by priests.
[2] Alb, or deacon's vestment.

choly eyes, at her earthly remains.

The clerk ran back to the church to fetch a *riza* for Father Anton. All looked at him in astonishment as he put it on. The smoke from the censor pervaded the room. The requiem mass had begun.

AN OCCASIONAL HOLIDAY.

I.

THE village of Kramariévka lies in a remote corner of the province of Kh—— and is surrounded by treeless steppes. The huts composing it are scattered along the banks of an extensive lake or backwater, fed by the river Dnieper. This village, the property of a landowner in times gone by, now enjoys entire liberty. It's emancipation from serfdom is eloquently attested by half-ruined huts whose sloping walls are supported by means of wooden props. Empty barns and threshing floors, whose surfaces cannot be swept clean for the simple reason that they are grown over thick with thistles and weeds, bear further witness to liberty, to that true liberty which, as is well known, always exists side by side with desperate poverty.

For the last three days the prospects of the villagers had been looking up. The heavy rain-clouds, which for several weeks in succession had been hanging over the land and ceaselessly pouring showers of rain upon the fields already saturated with moisture, now crossed the blue sky at less frequent intervals, and these, as if unable to endure the sun's bright rays, were hurrying away to hide themselves beneath the horizon. An oppressive feeling pervaded the air, the intensity of the sun's heat was suggestive of the dog-days rather than of May. Apparently the sun was desirous of atoning to the dwellers in Kramariévka for his long absence, and of making up for lost time by drying the fields and thereby enabling the peasant to commence the hay-harvest. What splendid grass had grown during these last three weeks, to be sure! It was as tall and thick as layer grass. Such a crop had not been seen by the peasants of Kramariévka for many a long year; it was to be hoped that the weather would hold up during the time required for the cutting and carting of it, for a premature return of the late diluvial storms would spoil the hay and render the peasants' labour fruitless—a worse catastrophe than if there had never been a prospect of a good crop. The rye crop also promised well; the green blades reared their heads tall and proud as autumn rushes; already the ears were forming, and the sun's warm rays would bring them to maturity. Joyous days were in store for the peasants if only God would send fine weather and preserve them from the ravages of the grasshopper.

This question of the harvest had
become a serious matter. For
six years running the *moujiks*
had scarcely done more than
reap that which they had sown.
But, notwithstanding these
failures, their sanguine natures
urged them to renew their
efforts at gaining a livelihood
from the niggardly soil. With
the desperation of savages they
would deprive their starving
children of the last morsels of
bread in order to sow the land
and reap, the following summer,
a fresh harvest of disappointment
as the fruit of their labour.
Many had at length abandoned
their agricultural pursuits in
disgust, and had set out in desperation, God knows whither, to
begin life afresh elsewhere. Some,
with hearts embittered, had abandoned the hateful, relentless land,
and, throwing in their lot with
fishermen, had for ever separated
themselves from husbandry ;
others wandered aimlessly into
distant inhospitable parts, but

were unable to keep away for long from their barren native soil. Half-starved and in rags, they returned home and poured forth lamentations over their allotments grown over, long since, with spear-grass, for that they possessed no *sokha* [1] wherewith to propitiate the cruel heart of their stepmother land, nor grain wherewith to bring her fresh sacrifices. Once upon a time the land had been own mother to the peasant, but of late years it had become stepmother.

An intolerable noise was going on in the yard of the *bátioushka's* parsonage. For five hundred yards around, the shrill tones of a woman's voice, accompanied at intervals by a male voice, the latter somewhat more subdued in pitch, could be heard. One of the persons engaged in this controversy was

---

[1] A sort of wooden plough used by the peasant.

the *matóushka* Agraphiéna Ivanovna—that self-same *matóushka* whose name the village women used in order to terrorise their children when the latter misbehaved themselves. " I'll take you to the *popadyá* [2] in a minute, and she'll eat you alive," a threat which as a rule had the desired effect ; the other person was her man-servant, Artem, a personage by no means so well-known as his mistress, but who nevertheless enjoyed a certain degree of popularity in the village. The *matóushka* was standing near a barn where the oats were stored, drawn up to her full height in the attitude of a person prepared to make a violent onslaught. Her bloodshot eyes seemed to start from their orbits with fury, her thin angular face wore an expression of deadly hatred ; the *matóushka* appeared to be out of her mind with rage. At such moments

---

[2] Another name for the priest's wife.

her expression would have furnished an admirable model for
an artist who desired to represent
a personification of fury. Artem
was standing in the barn beside
a bin half-filled with oats in the
traditional attitude of a man
conscious of his shortcomings.
In his left hand he held a quarter-
peck measure filled with corn,
and his cap, which he had taken
off out of respect for his mistress, hastily squeezed between
his fingers; his right hand was
employed scratching the back of
his head, a sure sign of an
uneasy conscience. His head
was hung down, and his eyes apparently strove to penetrate the
oats and gaze on the bottom of
the bin.

"Well, of course I know that
the horses are not mine but
yours; I only look after them
for you," said Artem, trying as
far as possible not to betray
any excitement.

"I only look after them for you,
indeed!" repeated the *matóushka,*

trying to mimic her servant's
voice, fully assured that she
would succeed in so doing by
speaking in a gruffer tone—
a performance, however, which
totally failed in producing any
effect. " We know very well how
you look after your master's
property. You destroy it instead
of taking care of it ! Christ
is not with you; you are a
man with no conscience ! You
imagine that I don't know
what becomes of all this corn;
you think that I am quite satisfied that you feed the horses
three times a day ? And what
about the *kabak ?* And what
is it that you squander in the
kabak but your master's property ? And then there are
those little devils of yours got
to be kept alive. O Lord ! how
hardly used I am ! Wherefore
dost Thou punish me thus ? "

This hardly-used person, receiving no answer to her in-
teresting question, banged the
door of the shed, adding em-

phatically, "Be hanged to you all!" as she disappeared into the house. The man remained standing by the corn-bin in his former attitude. Then he suddenly flung his peck measure on one side, straightened himself up, and gave vent to his pent-up feelings. His ire, no longer to be restrained, boiled up and showed itself on his swarthy, hairy countenance, his dark eyes glittered with wrath, and his fists were clenched.

"Be hanged to *you*, you old hag!" he almost groaned out between his teeth. . . . But then, as though suddenly remembering something, his fists became unclenched, and he thought of his hopelessly weak, wretched position; what did his curses signify to her! What was he? Had he not been taken on by his present employers almost as an act of charity: could he forget how he had implored them on his knees to take him on at a miserable

10

salary? Of a truth his position
came as near to slavery as could
be. No, Artem, you will do
best to calm yourself, for to-
morrow you may be kicked out,
and then you will have nothing
to take home to your four little
children—" young devils," as
the *matóushka* calls them, who,
as it is, are crying from hunger!
Artem's wrath therefore evapo-
rated, and he quietly went into
the stable. He fondly stroked
both the horses in turn ; they
turned their heads round and
seemed to look at him in a
friendly way. " Well, I am
not allowed to spoil you, my
dears," muttered Artem, addressing his horses. "Ah, my
little horses! I love you, although you do belong to the
pope," and meanwhile he continued stroking the horses' shiny
coats.

The *matóushka* returned to her
room completely overcome. One
might verily have believed that
she was an unfortunate being,

condemned by God Himself to a life of martyrdom : her face, that of a sufferer tortured, goaded, insulted without cause, was overspread with pallor, the blue lines of the overcharged veins stood out on her temples, her lips quivered nervously and seemed to be muttering abusive words, her thin hair straggled in disordered locks from underneath the cotton handkerchief which she wore on her head. Truly she was suffering, but it was not hard to see that her trouble was due to nothing but ill-temper. Notwithstanding her husband, to whom she had been married more than fifteen years, she felt a sense of loneliness and complete isolation. Father Leo was a mere child who required careful looking after : a person thoroughly unfit to be relied upon under any circumstances. His sole aspirations in life consisted of a taste for good eating and an aptitude for refreshing slumber. At this

very moment he was lying on
the sofa in his study, his lion-
like mane straggling over his
flabby countenance, and was
wrapped in entrancing . sleep.
Everything fell on her shoulders
in the management of domestic
affairs, and he counted for absolutely nothing. In the face of
such facts, could any one deny
that she was a martyr?

And pale-faced Agraféna Ivanovna very nearly wept from ill-
temper.

II.

ARTEM was fond of the priest's horses. This was perhaps because he himself had been the proprietor of a similar pair, not so very long ago. Nor was this all: he had lived in easy circumstances. Besides a pair of fine, well-fed oxen, he had owned a score of sheep, cows, pigs, and poultry; he had stored away grain, both barley and oats, in his own barn, and had partaken of substantial *bosrtch*[1] mixed with *kasha*[2] and dripping, at his own oak table, in his own house. His neat little wife Nástia used to keep house for him.

---

[1] A kind of soup.
[2] Buckwheat gruel.

Maxim Klad'ko, Artem's father, had handed him over a considerable amount of property at the time of his son's wedding. "See you, my son," said the old man to him then, "that you manage your affairs aright. Don't you squander your forefathers' property. Never let down the good name of your ancestors and father. The Klad'ko family were always good farmers."

Artem kept up the family reputation, and for six years laboured upon his allotment, sowing corn and barley—and scarcely reaping what he sowed. Nor was he alone in his misfortunes in this matter, the whole peasantry of the district suffered from similar misfortunes. And so each year some portion of Artem's stock-in-trade vanished. At first it was the sheep that had to be sold, then the oxen, then the horses. The loss of the cows was a terrible blow. Artem had by this time a family to support, and the children

could not do without milk. He
really had to keep back one cow
from the sale; but then came
winter, cold, hungry winter, and
the cow disappeared—the winter
had finished her off. Artem
looked around him and saw that
everything was bare, that the
very last trace of his father's
property had vanished, that his
wife was pining away, and that
his children were clamouring for
food. Artem's father was long
since dead, and there was no one
to whom he could apply for help.
One resource only remained—to
go out as a hired labourer and
earn sufficient to support his wife
and children through the winter.
Reviewing his position in the
world, Artem saw that he was a
different man to what he had
been. He had grown up ignorant of want; his handsome,
healthy countenance expressed
self-reliance and contentment;
his sturdy, muscular arms never
flagged at work; all jobs that
came into his hands soon got

paid for such a distinctive honour.
Now, of course, things would be
on quite a different footing. He
would scarcely be invited to par-
take of tea with them, nor would
any mention be made of the
wheat. He was then known as
Artem Maximovitch, but now it
was to be feared his name would
be converted into Artemka. On
presenting himself at the house,
the *bátioushka* did not come out
to see Artem, his corpulency
prevented him from troubling
himself with domestic matters;
his energies were devoted entirely
to questions concerning diet and
rest. The *matóushka* managed
all business affairs, and she it
was who interviewed Artem. At
first she did not even recog-
nise him, and asked what his
name was. Maxim Klad'ko's
son modestly recalled the occasion when he had drunk tea at
her house. She then remembered, and expressed surprise
that he had so come down in the
world, and feared that he had

not managed to keep up the property left him by his father. To
this Artem made no reply, but
came straight to the point. He
asked only for the miserable
salary of sixty roubles per annum.
Before starting on his errand, he
had reckoned that with sixty
roubles he would be able to buy
a yoke of oxen, and thereby perchance set his affairs aright
again. In addition to this, he
stipulated that rye biscuits should
be provided for the maintenance
of his family. The *matóushka* was
horrified at the sum demanded,
and expressed her opinion
that he must have lost his
senses. At a time when scores
of people were willing to work
for nothing, he dared to ask for
the exorbitant wage of sixty
roubles : perhaps .he thought he
had to do with a fool : or maybe
that she was already known
throughout the village as a luna-
tic ; or did he perchance suppose
that money fell from the heavens
into the pope's pocket ? Artem,

as a matter of fact, supposed none of these things, and merely wished to point out that there was a considerable difference between engaging any chance labourer, and a well known proprietor who was in uneasy circumstances. But this argument failed to impress the *matóushka*, and the situation was offered to him for the biscuits only, and a coat for the winter. Well does Artem remember the scene that followed.

"*Matóushka !* " said Artem, entreating her to listen to him, " if it were for my sake only, if I had not a wife and young children, if these children were not crying for food—do you think I would bargain with you thus ? I would work for you for my bread, for the husks of corn. But as I am a father, and have got to keep my family alive——"

Artem said this in such a tone of voice that had he been addressing a person with any heart, instead of the *matóushka*, he would most certainly have touched that heart.

"What is the use of your coming to me with this tale?" muttered the *matóushka*, as if she had never been possessed of a heart in her life. "Do you imagine that it is my fault that you have a wife and children? Am I to feed your children for you? I have plenty to do without them. What is it to me if they are crying for food? Maybe there are others also in the world who are hungry! There are generally plenty such! Do you suppose that I am going to feed them all?"

"*Matóushka!* I am not begging for alms. I offer to work for you as hard as I did for myself, and will look after your property as though it were my own. . . ."

"Ah, indeed! I beg of you that you will not do that! We all know how you have managed to look after your own property, and now you want to manage mine. What has become of your property, pray?"

At this the *matóushka* laughed ill-naturedly.

"Ah, but it was God, it was God who took it away from me! For these six years the crops have failed from drought and blight. Oh Lord, my God! Have I not slaved as hard as a pair of oxen? Is not my back nearly broken with fatigue?"

Artem by this time was in tears. He could no longer restrain himself now that his misfortunes were cast in his teeth. Had he squandered his property? Had he not always been a model proprietor? He had never allowed himself to be idle for a moment. He was at that time healthy and strong, and being endowed with an abundance of vigour, he worked from early dawn till late at night. He had earned for himself the name of *schoústri khosyáin.*[1] He was

---

[1] Industrious proprietor.

told that he was as good a man
as his father, and great things
were predicted for him in the
future. But these optimistic
prophecies were never fulfilled,
everything went wrong, and now
he was accused of carelessness,
of incapacity to preserve the property handed down to him. A
more cruel reproach than this it
would be difficult to imagine.
But Artem soon stopped weeping.
It suddenly occurred to him that
he was in the presence of a
brute who would never be moved
to pity by tears. In an instant
he changed his attitude and became, like his opponent, brutal.

" Well, look here : forty roubles
and biscuits ! I will not take a
penny less. Take it or leave it,
please yourself. Good-bye ! "

With this he abruptly turned
his back on her and went away.
He mentally resolved not to
remain in the *matóushka's* em-
ployment even if she agreed to
his terms. He felt that after
the humiliation he had suffered,

it would be disgraceful to accept
anything from her. He set off
with rapid steps to return to his
hut. His mind was in a dazed
condition. He was unable to
think about his plans or collect
his ideas. His heart was heavy
with despair. Had he found
himself at that moment standing
on the summit of a rocky cliff,
overlooking a swift deep stream
fringed with tender green rushes,
he would not have hesitated for
an instant, but would certainly
have hurled himself head foremost into the abyss. This would
be easier accomplished than the
return home empty-handed, and
the inevitable confession to be
made to his starving family that
he had found nothing wherewith
to satisfy their gnawing hunger.
Anyway, they were not as yet
plunged in despair, whereas his
arrival home must dispel the
last rays of hope. Presently,
however, Artem became aware
that some one was running after
him, and he heard the *matóushka's*

voice. The priest's wife, satisfied
that he would make no further
abatement in his demands, had
decided to agree to the terms he
proposed. She was well aware
that Artem might be exceedingly
useful to her, that he was no
mere adventurer, but a respec-
table person, well known in the
village. Artem's first impulse
was to take no notice of the
matóushka, but as there seemed
to be no other alternative, he
agreed to enter her service.

"She exasperates and breaks
me, I know it," thought he, but
nevertheless he stayed on with
her. This winter had been a
terrible one for poor Artem.
Formerly he was his own master
and knew well what it meant to
work on his own account. It
meant constant work, never sitting idle, but it meant also
husbanding his strength for the
morrow, as well as for the spring
and the summer. Here it was
different. The *matóushka* wanted
his strength for the present, for

just so long as he would remain
in her service ; Artem was, she
reckoned, good for one year, and
it was just for one year that she
required his services. When the
term agreed for had expired she
could get another man—a fresh
one. She did not care for keeping servants too long, and understood the art of extracting all
the work they were good for in
a twelvemonth. Her penetrating gaze followed her servant
every minute, ever on the alert
lest he should be without a job
for one instant. She could
always, if necessary, invent fresh
occupation ; her ingenuity in
this matter seemed inexhaus-
tible. Such duties as, for example, going down to the stream
in frosty weather to collect
rushes and bringing them back
on the sledge ; or sweeping the
snow fallen during the previous
night from the yard ; hacking
out lumps of ice from the river,
and carting them home to store
in the icehouse, should be per-

formed by the workman without his having to be reminded about them. But supposing a spare half-hour cropped up between the performance of the daily duties, the *matóushka* forthwith devised some fresh occupation. If, at a given moment, there chanced to be no regular work to hand, she would invent something perfectly superfluous; but sitting with idle hands could be in nowise tolerated—this was her fixed principle. In such a case she would order that the beds in the kitchen garden, frozen as hard as rock, be dug over; or she would transform the workman into cook, making him carry fuel into the kitchen, and place it on the hearth, or else cut up meat, or knead the dough. In fact, "idleness"—*i.e.*, necessary breathing-space — was not allowed in her establishment.

This all mattered but little to Artem. He knew the *matóushka* very well, and when he entered into the agreement with her he

understood that he was entering
upon a dire servitude, and that
for the space of a year he would
have to give all his strength
without reserve to his mistress.

But what he did not foresee
was that in his new situation
his every movement would be
accompanied by remarks which
wounded his self-respect as a
proprietor on his own account,
which, as he knew, had been so
highly estimated not long since
by the whole village. The priest's
wife looked upon her servants
as her deadly enemies. She
imagined herself encompassed at
every turn by evil-minded conspirators, who sought only how
to bring about her ruin. At
times she suspected that Artem
only did any work when her eye
was upon him, and that he slept
the remainder of his time; that
he stole half the horse-corn and
took it to the *kabak;* that, conspiring with the cook, Artem
carried away jugs full of milk to
his wife, and occasionally pieces

of roast meat, cooked for the *matóushka's* own table. Her eyesight seemed to be organised on principles quite peculiar to herself, for while it magnified the value paid by her to her servants, it seemed incapable of realising how it was that they possessed anything. Thus, when Artem took a peck of oats into the stables, the *matóushka* would come in before long and begin fumbling in the manger. She would then become furious.

"Ah, I thought so! You are at it already! Was that a peck you gave the horses? You mean to tell me that it was a peck? You shameless fellow! You steal in broad daylight! Yes, I know it well; I am simply being robbed, shamelessly robbed! I shall have nothing left me before long! What thievish cunning! You've managed to stow it away already somewhere. And so you want to set your affairs straight, do you? Yes, and you will soon do it at this rate! You will soon be a squire if you go on like this! Whereabouts in your establishment is the snug little corner where you stow away all the stolen goods? Yes, I should like to know where it is! I doubt not that there are plenty of good things there! I should open a shop! Do you think that it's all going to do you any good? Not a bit of it! Stolen goods never do any one any good!" &c., &c.

And so the *matóushka's* imagination continued to magnify the picture, until it assumed proportions and colouring altogether beyond the range of probability. She saw herself finally stripped of all her property, and wandering over the face of the earth an outcast. And thus she wanders from hut to hut, a bag in her hands, demanding alms in Christ's name. In the foreground is Artem surrounded by a flourishing family, making his fortune at a fabulous rate; his affairs have prospered, his wife grown stout, like one of the *matóushka's* fat pigs ; his children are proportionately fat for their ages, and unable to move from one place to another, &c. In fact, that Artem was realising to the utmost, the *matóushka's* own ideal of success in life.

The priest's wife never missed a chance of conjuring up such-like fantastic pictures in her mind. The chief share of accusations fell on Artem's shoulders, because his family was dependent upon him, which was, according to the *matóushka's* reasoning, an incentive to theft.

What specially enraged the *matóushka* more than anything else was to be answered. She expected that her torrents of abusive language would be listened to with befitting silence and even with gratitude.

During the winter months she gave her servants the cheapest possible sort of food. They occasionally had to be content with rye biscuits and *kvass*, or sour cabbage, or herrings, which were given by the parishioners as freewill offerings to the priest, and which therefore cost the *matóushka* nothing. More than once a protest was raised in the kitchen against such fare, and the right to hot dishes was claimed, and Artem even ventured to suggest that a glass of *vodka* would not be amiss as a recompense for his labours. The just indignation of the *matóushka* at such proposals was a thing to be seen.

"I feed you badly, do I? And what did you get at home, I should like to know? You had to make shift with peeled barley mixed with sand. And you were ready to sell your souls for a rotten herring. In my house you are growing fat, and yet you clamour for more. You can just clear out of it, all of you, if you don't like it. I am not going to stand on any ceremony with you. Why, there's Michael Zabára longing to enter my

service, one-eyed Feódka im-
plores me by heaven to take
him on for his keep alone, and
Palàshka Fedotíkhina — by no
means a bad girl—is ready to
come to me at any moment.
Yes, there are plenty of them,
indeed. You can all go your
ways if you like, and beg your
bread. You had better go and
found a colony of beggars! Ah,
you have come to your senses
now, you shameless people!
You do not know your true
value! You are worth about a
halfpenny. That's what I think
of you. . . ."

The *matóushka* expressed herself even more forcibly than this,
and the inhabitants of the kitchen
were reduced to silence. Each
of them really believed that their
mistress would think nothing of
turning them out then and there
without wages. But as soon as
the *matóushka's* back was turned,
the servants would all repeat, as
though with one consent, the
following words:

"May you never prosper, either in this world or in the next, you thrice cursed extortioner."

This was the state of affairs in the *bátioushka's* household towards the beginning of spring.

HI, you there, Matrióna! You must get up earlier to-morrow morning, at two o'clock! No more idling in bed till four o'clock. I want you to go to work in the fields with Artem."

These words were addressed by the *matóushka* to her servant, Matrióna, just as the latter was retiring for the night. It was already eleven o'clock—a very late hour according to rustic notions. Matrióna had only just finished cleaning up the crockery and feeding her mistress's two pet dogs—animals of doubtful pedigree—and she was so worn-out with fatigue that she could scarcely keep on her legs. As a

matter of fact she was already
half asleep, her senses were
dulled with weariness and her
eyelids heavy. But the *matoushka's* orders made her start up,
and she opened her big eyes
wide, and fixed them in astonishment upon her mistress. The
thought at once occurred to her
that she had entered the *matoushka's* service as housemaid, it being
understood that she was only to
undertake indoor work. By what
right, then, was she suddenly to
be ordered out to work in the
fields ? Although Matrióna made
no remark in reply, the penetrating gaze of the *matoushka* was
able to perceive the train of
reasoning which was going on in
her servant's mind.

" Well, what do you stand
staring there like an owl for ?
Maybe you don't wish to get up,
eh ? You like to stay in your
warm, comfortable bed ? Hand-
ling the rake, perhaps, seems to
you hard work. You think that
a housemaid is not called upon

to do field work. Is that it?
Very well, you just try it on!
Mind that out you go, if you dis-
obey me, and never let me see
your face again! Do you understand me? Go along! And take
care that I do not find you asleep
out in the field, for I know your
idle ways! You are always on
the look out for an opportunity
of getting under the cart and
snoring!"

Matrióna answered nothing,
but wearily went on her way to
bed.

On the following day, before
the first rays of dawn had appeared, a cart drawn by two
horses, containing a scythe and
hay-rakes, left the gates of the
bátioushka's yard. In it were
seated Artem and Matrióna.
Artem looked fresh and well.
He was accustomed to getting
up in the middle of the night in
order to see if the horses wanted
feeding; Matrióna still appeared
to be half asleep, for it was not
more than two o'clock in the

morning. The road leading through the village was enshrouded in mist which covered the roofs of the huts, the narrow stream, and the church belfry. Here and there in the vault of the skies, stars were faintly shining through the mist; as though sensible of the approach of dawn, the blackness of the night became more intense than ever; the two horses pricked up their ears as they timidly advanced along the dark road. The fresh breeze of dawn saturated with moisture was blowing; cocks were crowing in the yards of the peasants, and their owners were just beginning to think about getting up.

"Whose cart and horses can that be, I wonder, going out so early to work?" asked a *moujik*, rubbing his eyes heavy with sleep.

"It must be the priest's, I suppose," answered his wife.

"Busy folks, the priest's servants, to be up so early!" remarked the *moujik*.

" Ah, and you'd be busy too if you were compelled to work for that cursed hag," thought Artem, as he passed by. Matrióna heard nothing of these remarks, she was lying in the bottom of the cart fast asleep.

The village was at length left behind, and the cart turned into the fields. The darkness gradually became less intense, the stars twinkled more faintly, and a streak of dawn appeared. The pale light revealed grassy plains as far as the eye could reach. The morning breeze softly swept over the thick green grass. Artem looked at the scene around him, and his face seemed to light up with pleasure. It was a long time since he had seen such a pleasant picture. The thick green grass promised an abundant hay crop, such as the dwellers in Kramariévka had longed for for many a year. The rye was half a foot high. The spring wheat, barley, and oats were sprouting in a most promising manner.

" God forbid that the crops
should be burnt up by drought,
or that locusts, hail, or other
pestilences should destroy them!
What rejoicings there will then
be among the peasants ! " muttered Artem to himself, glancing
around at the boundless steppes,
and devoutly making the sign of
the cross. The thought of the
good time coming brought joy to
Artem's heart, but an instant
later his brow became furrowed.
Thoughts suddenly occurred to
him which filled his heart with
inexpressible anguish, and he
hung down his head and ceased
admiring the lovely landscape
that lay before his eyes. He
remembered that it would be
impossible for him to take any
part in the coming rejoicings,
that he would have to look
on as a mere outsider at the
good fortune of others. For five
years he had sown the land, and
had run through all his fortune ;
the sixth year, when he had
become a beggar and thrown up

his business, having nothing wherewith to sow his crops, as though purposely, God had sent this good fortune to men. Such reflections caused feelings of jealousy and hatred to enter his mind. Jealousy is said to be a sin. But seeing God had wronged him, how could he help feeling thus ?

What a fine crop of hay there was on the glebe land ! How thick and green it had grown ! It was a pleasure to see such grass ! The sun was by this time fully risen, the larks were flying about, a seagull hovering over the plain had disappeared from sight a minute later. Artem set to work with his scythe in a half-hearted manner, Matrióna following him with her rake in a leisurely fashion. Bordering on the glebe land lay the fields belonging to the squire, which extended in all directions for a considerable distance and occupied about twenty-five thousand acres. Not far from where

Artem was at work, a large party of labourers were engaged in mowing the grass on the squire's land. These all had sunburnt faces and wore home-made hats of barley straw, shirts well patched, and baggy trousers of variegated patterns. They were followed by women and young girls dressed in gaudy-coloured petticoats. Artem could tell by the snatches of conversation which he heard, that these people came from the province of Poltáva, and leaning for a moment on the handles of his scythe, he addressed the man who was nearest to him—

"You are strangers here, I expect?" asked he, resuming his work with the scythe.

"Yes, we are Poltávtsi, all of us," answered the young fellow to whom the question was addressed, stopping work for a moment.

"Why have you come to these parts?"

"Ah, you may well ask why,"

answered the youth, in a tone of vexation.

" How's that ? "

" Why, look here : we've come from Poltáva, forty-two men of us. It took us nearly a fortnight to get here. By the time we arrived, we were so worn out and hard up for cash, that we came near to calling out for help. Your land is a poor one, and the people all seem different to ours. Being in foreign parts all alone is as bad as being lost in a thick wood. We came across a man who said to us, ' I'll hire you all till the Feast of the Intercession at the rate of one hundred roubles for each man and sixty for each woman.' Well, there were some of our company who had worked in these parts before, and we asked their opinion. ' We never found prices so good in former years. We got ninety-five roubles one year and ninety another, so you will do well to close with this man, for it's a good price.' So we agreed with him. And as things have turned out, it seems we have given away our services. Just look at this hay! . . . and see what a harvest there will be. We have just heard that men are getting one and a half roubles a day for hay-making, and that prices will go up again as the rye ripens. Indeed, I believe they'll go to two and a half or even three; and the women even are getting a rouble a day—just fancy that! I think we have been pretty well taken in."

"Bad luck to those fellows who advised us," muttered another native of Poltáva, a man with a gloomy, ill-natured countenance.

"May you get the pip, abusing us like that!" exclaimed an elderly Poltáva peasant who wore long moustaches and bore an extraordinary resemblance to the portrait of Mazeppa as he is represented on cheap engravings. "How were we to know that things would turn out as they have?"

"Whether you knew or not, it is certain that we have got to slave away till the feast of the Intercession for one hundred roubles, when we might be earning just twice that amount."

"Ah, you brainless southerners!" shouted a voice at the sound of which all the men looked round. These words were spoken by a tall, broad-shouldered *moujik*, whose countenance was pitted with smallpox and who wore a clipped beard. His head was covered by a felt hat, the brim of which had become bent downwards by the action of time. He had a straightforward, manly expression, and the good-natured tone in which he spoke betrayed a slight shade of irony. He spoke smoothly and fluently in the sing-song manner of Great Russian natives.

"Listen to me, I tell you! What's the good of your going on like that at each other? How were they to know? Do you

suppose that a man is such a
fool as to harm himself? You
must remember that they who
advised us to close with the offer
of one hundred roubles did the
same thing themselves! You
listen to *my* advice now!"

"Sss . . . you Yaroslavl goat!
Who made you a leader?" asked
the Poltáva men with unfeigned
scorn; nevertheless they left
their scythes and collected
around the "Yaroslavl goat,"
ready to listen to what he had
to say.

"Now then, mind you tell us
something worth listening to,"
condescendingly remarked several
of the audience.

"Well, listen to me!" continued the Yaroslavl man in a
free and easy tone. "Tell me,
you dull-headed southerners,
whether it is we who are more
in need of the landlord, or the
landlord of us, at this present
moment. Eh, what have you
got to say to that?"

The Poltáva men pondered

over this question in solemn silence.

"Why, we of course are more useful to him," continued the man from Yaroslavl, without waiting for their answer; "because you see what the grass is like—the weather is scorching hot, and every day lost means loss of money to the landowner. Each day lost costs him at least a thousand roubles. Therefore it follows that he ought to value our services accordingly."

"Quite right!" rejoined the audience unanimously.

"Very well. So we are agreed on that point. In fact we have got him in our hands, and can do what we like with him!"

"So we can," interrupted the men from Poltáva again.

"So we can," repeated the sharp-witted northerner, mimicking his listeners. "And if that's so, what then?"

The Yaroslavl peasant was evidently well pleased with his inventive talent and his intellectual superiority over the Poltáva men; and this circumstance annoyed one of the latter, namely him who bore a resemblance to Mazeppa.

"Stop, you goat-bearded fellow!" exclaimed this man, angrily interrupting the orator. "Do you think we can't see what you are driving at? Where's your conscience? Maybe it's as goat-like as your beard."

"Ha—ha—ha!" The speaker burst out into a loud, sonorous laugh. "That's it, is it! That's your idea! You silly southerner! So we are to lose our earnings to satisfy our consciences! Do you suppose he troubles about his conscience because he pays us a rouble, when others are getting a rouble and a half? What sort of conscience do you call that? What's the good of hair-splitting about conscience? Throw down your scythes, my friends. Let him see that we must be paid as the others are

being paid. . . . Why should we
lose that which is our due?
This is our chance of good luck :
it comes but rarely ! How many
years have we looked in vain
for it ? Conscience—rubbish ! "
And with these words the Yaroslavl peasant laid down his
scythe and sat down, stretching
out his legs encased and bound
round with rags.

The Poltáva men stopped
work and stood about in silence,
evidently undecided what to
do.

" Don't you listen to him, boys.
Let him kick up a row if he's
discontented," said a peasant
"with a conscience." " Shall we
be acting aright if we fail to
keep our word ? "

This good counsel was clearly
as unheeded as the voice of one
crying in the wilderness. Several
of the southerners had seated
themselves on the ground without saying a word; others as
yet undecided, were discussing
the situation among themselves.

They all at length came to the
conclusion that they were each
entitled to receive their due.
The pleasant idea of possibly
earning two hundred roubles
instead of half that sum, passed
through the minds of each of
them, and gradually all the party
of reapers seated themselves in
a group around the Yaroslavl
agitator.

The women seated themselves
down first without any further
discussion. The agitator's idea
seemed so very advantageous.
The only man who did not sit
down with the others was the
" man with the conscience ; "
but even he had stopped work,
and was leaning on his scythe
and reviewing the situation in
his mind.

" What are you puzzling your
head over, you wiseacre ? Come
and sit down and shut up work !
You won't be called upon to
answer for our doings," said the
agitator, in a convincing manner.

" It's against my conscience,

it is indeed!" said the peasant,
still unconvinced, but at the
same time taking his seat on
the grass in a hesitating manner,
and remaining at some little
distance from the other members
of the company, as though avoid-
ing all contact with them.

"Ha, ha! it's against your
conscience, is it? and still you
give up work!" ironically remarked one of the women.

"But what can I do, left all
alone as I am?" angrily rejoined
the peasant. "I don't want to
lose what's my due! All I say
is, that this does not seem to me
right, and this I shall always
maintain."

"So much the better!" care-
lessly remarked the Yaroslavl
man, highly delighted that the
whole company was now won
over to his views. "Let's fold
our arms, stretch out our legs,
and sit and whistle!"

Suiting his action to his words
the agitator commenced whistling, to the great delight of the

female portion of the party. All the company were in high spirits. At this juncture, however, a horseman appeared on the dusty road at no great distance. He was a broadly-built fellow with reddish beard and whiskers, and his eyes were small grey, and furtive. He had the habit of holding his head on one side, and from this circumstance had earned the nickname of "the off-side horse." He was dressed in check trousers, a short coat of yellowish tint, and a peaked cap. His face and clothes were completely covered with dust. He was riding as fast as he could urge on his wearied steed with the riding-whip. He was the farm bailiff, and it was his duty to look after the reapers and keep them up to their work. He kept riding from one party of workers to the next; there were in all, forty parties of fifty workers each, employed at distances of about six hundred yards from each other.

"Hullo, you fellows! What

are you sitting there for? What does this mean? Look alive, get to work!" shouted the bailiff in a hoarse voice, and at the same time flourishing his whip in such an irate manner that it whistled as it cut through the air. However, none of the party moved from their places.

"What are you sitting there for, I ask you? Have you all gone stone deaf?"—the bailiff here added a few of his favourite violent expressions.

"What are you shouting at us for? We want our dinner, it's time for dinner! That's why we've sat down!" answered one of the party.

"You must have gone mad, all of you!" cried out the bailiff in a rage—"wanting your dinner when the sun has hardly risen!"

"Anyway we shall not do any work till we have had our dinner!"

The bailiff was in doubt as to what this meant. But a moment later he seemed to grasp the situation. He prided himself on being a "cunning dog," and understood, from the manner in which the men spoke, there was something of an unusual nature going on. He had a very keen eye for all such matters, and instantly the word "strike" occurred to his mind. Having had experience in such affairs he knew the best course to pursue, and therefore changed his tone and assumed a gentle manner which ill suited his fox-like countenance.

"Hm!—I see!" muttered the bailiff as though to himself. "Very well, if you wish for your dinner, I will order it."

He turned his horse's head and started off again at full speed. A few minutes later the kettle for boiling the *kasha* was brought, cooking operations were commenced, and dinner was soon ready. The labourers brought out their spoons, and sat down with their soup-dishes in front of them. They all wore a stubborn and silent air. The Yaroslavl peasant alone of the party still remained smiling, and occasionally made jokes addressed chiefly to the women, who seemed to understand him better than the men. The conspirators evidently were in doubt as to what they were to do next, or what would come of the affair; but the northerner knew very well that the others would follow his lead. They began to eat in an indolent fashion, for, to tell the truth, no one was hungry, as they had only just had breakfast.

"*Tfou!*" suddenly ejaculated the Yaroslavl peasant, spitting. "Do they call this *kasha*? Is this buckwheat? What's this, boys? He has fed his pigs with the buckwheat, and this is what they have left! Put down your spoons, boys! We won't work for such *kasha* as this!"

With these words, he threw aside his spoon and turned his bowl of *kasha* upside down. The miserable thin liquid trickled

over the grass. A roar of laughter
was raised at this, and the *kasha*
from the other basins was dealt
with in a similar unceremonious
fashion. It was easy to see that
things were beginning to take a
serious turn.

The bailiff knitted his brows;
his hands were trembling with
rage; but he did not lose his self-
control, and wisely maintained
silence. He knew full well that
if he opened his mouth it would
be to use abusive language. He
went up to the kettle with an air
of constrained calmness, and took
a spoonful of the *kasha* and tried
it. There was certainly no fault
to be found with the buckwheat;
in fact, there could be no doubt
whatever now as to the real
cause of the discontent.

" What does this mean? You
don't want to do any more work?
Is that it? Why do you say
nothing? I must speak about
this to the squire."

" All right; tell him all that's
happened," answered the strikers
in a resolute manner.

The bailiff angrily spat on the ground, then mounted his horse and galloped off in the direction of the village to see the squire. In the meanwhile the workmen belonging to another neighbouring party saw from afar off that something of an unusual nature was occurring. Directly after the bailiff had ridden off, an envoy arrived from the other labourers to ask what was the matter. These latter, overcome by curiosity, had almost given up their work—they hardly felt inclined for it at present; besides which, the bailiff was not to be seen, so that there was no object in doing anything.

The conspirators pulled out their pipes, filled them up with "twist," and began smoking. The strikers were seated about in a free-and-easy fashion, and appeared by no means anxious, and were even engaged in discussing outside events. They had by this time quite accustomed themselves to their new situation. More than half an hour had thus passed away, when a huge cloud of dust was seen arising in the distance towards the village. Horsemen gradually became visible, and in the rear of the cavalcade appeared the squire's well-appointed gig.

"I say, boys, what a cloud of dust we've managed to knock up!" remarked the ringleader in a jaunty tone of voice.

The horsemen approached. Among them were the bailiffs, outriders, engineer, and others; in fact, the whole staff of the squire's estate management. Among them was the head agent, a fat German, whose vocabulary of Russian words did not extend beyond those of a violent character.

"What's this?" "What are you up to?" "You brainless *moujiks!*" "Do you know what this will do for you?" "You'll certainly get sent to Siberia!" "The law punishes such an offence with penal servitude!"

" This is a revolt — you are mutineers ! "

The bailiffs kept shouting out suchlike words, all talking at the same time; the agent, however, only grew redder and angrier, sincerely regretting his inability to speak to the men. But still the strikers remained perfectly indifferent to all that was being said to them, and continued conversing among themselves.

The squire then came up. He was a medium-sized man of good build, about forty years old ; his face was clean shaven, and his black hair closely cropped. He wore a light-coloured summer suit, and a hat made of wood shavings, with the brim turned downwards. His manner was calm and dignified. He was considered to be the most highly cultured man in the whole district, and as a local magnate had won for himself general popularity. He had a very good library, and subscribed to numerous magazines and papers, the back numbers of which he kept in elegant bindings and port-folios. His reputation among the peasants was that of an easy-going, pleasant man. He never allowed himself to speak brusquely to a peasant, always made a point of addressing his social inferiors in the second person plural, and responded to those who saluted him by taking off his hat and graciously bowing his head. His highly sensitive nature abhorred the use of coarse words and strong expressions, and his agents and bailiffs had very strict orders to treat the workmen with proper considera-tion.

The squire descended from his gig, and slowly approached the group of labourers. At this the bailiffs were silent, and the men stood up and took off their hats.

" I hear, sirs, that you are discontented with the *kasha* sup-plied you. Is this the case ? " He asked this question in an easy tone of voice, and with unaffected dignity. Receiving no answer, he continued: "I am very glad to think that this is not true, for, were it so, I should consider myself wronged, for it is well known throughout the district that the food I supply is excellent. I am bound to suppose that there is some other cause than this for your conduct —that you wish to break your contract. . . ."

"We never made any contract . . . ." timidly suggested some one.

The calm, dignified manner in which the squire spoke seemed to somewhat confuse the conspirators. They were already beginning to feel that they were in the wrong. The astute Yaroslavl man saw this, and therefore made ready to address a speech on behalf of his fellows.

"Well . . . certainly no formal contract has been signed; but you made a bargain which is binding on your consciences.

However, I am well aware that the voice of conscience has no influence in the action of some people! . . ." continued the squire, with a contemptuous smile on his face. "What is it that you want from me?"

The Yaroslavl man came forward.

"We want nothing from your excellency. We only want you to settle up with us," said he, in a bold tone of voice.

The Poltáva men looked at each other anxiously. This statement evidently surprised them.

"What do you mean—settle up with you?" asked the squire, with a shade of anxiety in his voice. He really was beginning to feel rather uncomfortable. This affair might possibly cost him several thousand roubles. A huge strip of grass land would remain unmown if he paid off this party. For the last three days it had been impossible to engage any fresh hands—they were all busy; and in the mean-

while the sun was pitilessly
scorching the earth.   Another
day, and the grass must be burnt
up and become useless.

"Yes, sir, that's what we want
—our account," respectfully continued the Yaroslavl man.   "You
wish as we do, that everything
should be done fairly.   At the
present moment reapers are
earning a rouble and a half, and
the women a rouble; we shall go
to a place where we can get that
price.   We shall not have to go
far, for there are plenty who will
take us; so that we must ask
you for our wages."

"Ah! I see you wish to cause
me an enormous loss of money.
Well, we'll see about that.   You
forget, however, that I am in
possession of your papers, and
that without your papers no one
will hire you.   I decline either
to give up your papers or to
settle your wages. So, my friends,
you see you have been a little bit
hasty in your calculation!"

"Oh no, sir; we thought all

about that! It's not we who have made the mistake!" answered the leader of the strike in a respectful tone, but with a shade of irony in his voice. "We shall not trouble ourselves about your keeping our papers; we shall leave you all the same. People who really want more hands don't trouble much about their papers. . . . This is rather an important time. . . ."

"But suppose that I sue you for damages? . . ."

" You'll get nothing, for there's nothing to get!" was the reply.

The squire, notwithstanding his assumed calmness of manner, found it necessary to wipe his forehead with his handkerchief. He had used up all the arguments at his disposal. Time was passing. Every hour lost meant a loss of hundreds of roubles. He felt that an understanding must be arrived at, at any cost. It required but little arithmetic to come to the conclusion that it would be far better to offer an increased wage at the price then prevailing, rather than lose the services of a whole party of workmen.

"How much do you want?" asked the squire.

"The same as the others are getting—a rouble and a half for the men and a rouble for the women."

"All right; but I shall make you sign a contract, and then if . . ."

"We won't have any contract, it does not suit us. . . . The price will go up again! . . ."

"Indeed? I have already ten parties working at this price, and you wish me to make an exception in your favour. . . . Very well, then, I shall find men elsewhere."

"We don't know anything about the other parties, . . . but see over there."

The squire glanced in the direction of the other party. He could see that work had already ceased with them also, and the men were sitting down. This spectacle finally exhausted his patience, and he could scarcely restrain himself from freely giving vent to his feelings.

"I much regret that I have wasted words and reasonable propositions on men who are only worthy of contempt," said the squire, in tones of unfeigned disgust, although it was on the tip of his tongue to call them scamps, swindlers, &c. He got into his gig and drove off to the next party in a great rage. His herd of employés, with a look of great anxiety on their faces, galloped after him.

"Now, then, Mr. '*barin*,'[1] you'll have to take care of your money, else it'll be all slipping away from you. What does it matter to him if he makes a few hundreds less out of us! But he would like to pocket them if he could! That's the way that money is made! . . ."

---

[1] Gentleman.

Such were the sentiments expressed by the strikers after the squire's departure. A quarter of an hour later a bailiff dashed up on horseback.

"Hullo you there! Get to work! Look alive! You'll be paid at the market price for labour! But mind, you must work for it! Now, then, try and make up what you've lost this morning."

IV.

ARTEM and Matrióna did very little mowing that day. They worked on in a listless manner, and the scythe hardly seemed to make any impression on the grass. They stopped at frequent intervals, laying down their implements, and seated themselves on the ground, concentrating all their attention upon the scene above described. Anxiously listening to what was being said, they lost not a single word, but carefully followed the progress of events in order to see how the affair would end. Artem looked sullen, and took no notice of Matrióna's impatient remarks, but his outward demeanour only disguised a feeling of triumphant joy which every moment gained in force : he felt that his destiny was entirely dependent upon the successful result of the strikers' action. As soon as the final issue at stake between the men and their employer was settled, he got up and heaved a deep sigh, like a man who, after incessant labour, has at length successfully terminated a difficult task.

" It's time to go home ! " said he, turning to Matrióna. " We've done enough of this work at a halfpenny a day."

" Yes, we have indeed ! " rejoined Matrióna, without hesitation. " We are as good as they are."

So saying, she tossed her head with unfeigned pride, as if she really was some one of no small importance. This attitude suited her admirably, so much so, that any observer might have supposed that under her coarse sunburnt skin flowed a dash of blue blood. Nevertheless, it was known for a certainty that she was the daughter, granddaughter and great - granddaughter of common peasants.

Artem joyfully urged on the horses. All the way home he kept singing and winking at Matrióna, to the surprise of the latter. His jovial aspect also caused wonder to those he met on the road, as well as to the peasants at work on the meadows adjoining the roadway. They knew that Artem was a morose man. True it was that formerly he had had a reputation as a good-natured, jolly sort of a fellow, but after misfortune had overtaken him he seemed to lose all his high spirits, and became silent and gloomy. To-day, however, he suddenly seemed to regain his former spirits.

The early return of the priest's servants from work was the cause of surprise to all who saw them. It seemed to every one a violation of the *matóushka's* rule that her servants should be the first to arrive at work and the last to leave it. But the sun was only beginning to descend in the skies, and no one had thought of going home yet.

"Now, Matrióna, mind you behave yourself properly."

"You may be sure of that," replied Matrióna.

"All right. Don't you forget, though. We don't intend to give up what is our due. Things will not right themselves all at once, but by degrees! . . . So take care that you don't get frightened. . . . Ah, well I know you women—as soon as anything happens, you are ready to turn tail. . . . She is hag enough to frighten any one, I know, . . . a veritable she-devil."

"Oh, I'm not afraid of her!" answered Matrióna, in a tone expressive of self-confidence.

Artem began singing and

whistling in a careless manner whilst the well-nourished priest's horses trotted through the village. He felt very cheerful. "There will be a fine scene here presently! How the old hag will fume!" thought he, with malignant joy, and pictured to himself the scene of the *matóushka* with dishevelled hair and mad with rage, while he, Artem, stood before her with his cap on his head, and smiling ironically. However, nothing of the sort happened, much to Artem's surprise.

"What's brought you home so early?" asked the priest's wife, without even looking at Artem.

"We had had enough of it! We started out very early; even the village cocks were still asleep!" replied Artem, in a free-and-easy manner. He himself even felt surprise at the tone in which he addressed the *matóushka*. But this manner soon gave place to a more subdued tone; his voice trembled and became lower.

"Have you done much mowing?" asked the *matóushka*.

"A fair amount, about an acre!"

"H'm . . . an acre! I must say you are fine sort of haymakers!" muttered the priest's wife, almost to herself; and without further remark she left the room, much to the surprise of Artem and Matrióna.

The *matóushka's* manner seemed strange, and unlike her ordinary self. On this occasion, however, she walked about the room with a determined, self-contained look on her countenance, her thoughts evidently concentrated on one all-absorbing subject. To judge by her appearance, one might have supposed that she was trying to find her way out of some grave difficulty which suddenly threatened to upset the even tenor of her life. She went to the door leading to Father Leo's study, and knocked.

14

"Leo! Wake up! I want you!"

"What's the matter now?" replied the voice of one apparently awaking from sleep.

"I want you! There's important business," repeated the *matóushka*.

It should be observed that however angry the *matóushka* might be with her husband, she always addressed him in a quiet manner. She recognised the importance of not disturbing his rest. Father Leo got up quickly, for he knew from his wife's manner that this was no ordinary affair. He entered the sitting-room, half asleep and without his coat on. A council of war was then held.

"You've no idea of all that's going on while you are quietly sleeping!" commenced the *matóushka*.

"What's happened?" asked Father Leo in a frightened tone of voice.

"What has happened is simply

this : the squire's men have declined to work unless they are
promised higher wages. The
trouble first began with one
party of men, and soon spread to
the rest. The bailiff Matvei has
been round here and told me all
about it. He says this affair will
cost the squire several thousands.
. . . That is what has happened ! "

" I don't quite see how it affects
us," remarked Father Leo.

" Why, do you suppose that
our people will not take advantage of this ? I can tell you that
they have had a grudge against
us for a long time, and just now
is their chance of paying us out ;
they know very well that hands
are scarce—all are busy at work,
and that high wages are being
paid everywhere. It is in their
power to put us in a pretty fix, by
throwing up work and leaving us
to our own devices ! "

" Rubbish ! " . . . said Father
Leo, trying to dispel his wife's
forebodings. " You need not

trouble your head about that. I've got their passports; you don't suppose I should be such a fool as to give them up."

"Ah, you don't understand what you are talking about," angrily interrupted the *matóushka*. "Passports have nothing to do with the matter as things now stand. Employers are eagerly searching for hands throughout the district. What do they care about passports so long as they can find fresh hands. . . . We shall simply be left in the lurch with their passports. . . ."

"Well, what's to be done?" anxiously asked the priest.

"We must simply do all we can to keep on good terms with them. I feel sure that they want to pick a quarrel about something. Especially that fellow Artem: he is a regular good-for-nothing! I know what he has got on his mind. The moment I looked at him to-day, I guessed what was up. . . . Now I'll tell you what you must do: it wouldn't

come well from me, it would be
too sudden : you know I've never
spoilt my servants, so it would
look queer. . . . You just call
Artem in, and give him a good
glass of *vodka*, and talk to him a
bit, you know, . . . something
about the spring beginning, eh !
. . . or that he must fortify himself for the long summer days
coming. . . . You can do it better
than I, because you know how to
talk. But mind you put on your
coat first, otherwise it will look
strange. Although he's only
a workman, still it wouldn't
do. He will tell the others all
about it. . . . By the way, I
nearly forgot to tell you, I sent
them off to work very early this
morning, and so they are rather
sulky. So just say that you
chanced to learn of this, and
were much annoyed about it, and
that in future you will not let
such a thing happen again."

Father Leo quite agreed that
he ought to put on his coat—he
even went further than this, and

arrayed himself in his cassock,
thus assuming an air of greater
solemnity than the occasion demanded. Matrióna was sent to
fetch Artem. With curiosity
characteristic of her sex, she had
been unable to resist the tempta-
tion of applying her ear to the
keyhole of the door leading to the
sitting-room, and had by this
means managed to catch every
word of the foregoing conversation. She found Artem in the
stable at his favourite occupation
—looking after the horses.

"I say, Artem! Come along
and have some *vodka!*" said
Matrióna to him so abruptly that
she made him start.

"What do you mean?" asked
Artem surprised.

"A good glass, I promise you!
I don't suppose that the *bátioushka*
and the *matóushka* drink bad
vodka."

"Have you gone mad? What
are you talking about the *bátioushka's vodka?* I shouldn't be
surprised if you haven't stolen a
bottle."

"Oh no, I haven't; besides which, I never drink *vodka!* You don't imagine that I would steal it for your benefit, do you?" said Matrióna in a tone of virtuous indignation, just as though she had never taken advantage of a quiet moment down in the cellar to have a taste of the *matóushka's* favourite apricot jam. But she was of a forgiving disposition, and so continued:

"The *matóushka* has heard all about the strike, and is afraid that we shall follow their example. . . . Well, I heard her telling the *bátioushka.* She said, 'Send for Artem and treat him to a drink, for we must keep him in good humour.' . . . So hurry up! The *bátioushka* is waiting for you, in his best cassock, just as if he were going to mass!"

At this Matrióna smiled maliciously.

"I won't refuse his *vodka!* It's about time he gave me some—he owes me a good glass for my work! . . . And mind you bring out a good big glass" (this was said aside to Matrióna). "But it's rather late in the day for them to think about doing me a good turn. . . ."

Artem put down the brush which he held in his hand, and put on his worn-out, patched overcoat (for seeing that his master was to receive him dressed in his cassock, it would scarcely be suitable for Artem to appear in his shirt-sleeves), and left the stable. As they crossed the yard, Matrióna continued, in a confidential whisper, lest she should be overheard :

"The *matóushka* said: 'That fellow Artem is a regular scoundrel, I can see through him.'"

Matrióna was interrupted at this point, for just then the *matóushka's* head appeared at one of the windows of the corridor. Matrióna hastily left Artem and ran off to find a "good big glass" for the *vodka*. She evidently had no very high opinion of her mistress's powers of observation ; for

just as she had got hold of a decanter filled with the *vodka* usually
supplied at table, and a large
wine-glass used by the *bátioushka*
before meals, the priest's wife
stopped her.

" Stop, you idiot, where are
you off to in such a hurry? You
ought to ask me first. Take
this ! "

And the *matóushka* pointed to
a bottle of a commoner description ; the *vodka* it contained was
five degrees lower than that used
at the *matóushka's* table. This
lesser degree of alcoholic strength
was arrived at by the simple pro-
cess of adding water ; bottles of
this description are known under
the appellation of the " people's
brand " : the liquid they contain
may likewise be called the " people's," so that the glass used in
the consumption of such liquor
should be of a corresponding
kind. This latter article was
apparently of enormous dimensions, but by reason of its thick
sides and substantial bottom, its

capacity was by no means proportionate to its size. But this was in accordance with the *matóushka's* theory of domestic economy.

Artem entered the sitting-room, and remained standing with his hat in his hand, while the other was engaged in carefully stroking his hair and moustaches. He looked brighter and more at his ease than usual. Father Leo entered the room from his study arrayed in his cassock, his long hair carefully combed out, in contrast to his usual unkempt appearance. As a rule, he only performed this operation when about to conduct divine service, or to administer extreme unction, or suchlike solemn duties. Artem bowed as the priest entered, and received Father Leo's blessing.

"Good-day to you, Artem Maximovitch!" began Father Leo in an amicable tone of voice. "I hope you are quite well?"

"O-ho!" thought Artem: "I am 'Maximovitch' now!" He

knew, however, that the priest was a very mild-mannered man, but he felt somewhat taken aback by being addressed in the ceremonious style to which, in times gone by, he had been accustomed.

" Pretty well, thank God . . . with your prayers ! " answered Artem aloud, although he had his doubts as to whether Father Leo ever did pray for him.

" You've been out haymaking to-day, I hear ? "

" Yes."

" Tell me, pray, what happened out there. What's all this tale I hear about the squire's men? Are they dissatisfied ? "

" The Lord only knows them. . . . What have they been doing ? Has there been any difficulty ? I have heard nothing of it ! " answered Artem, in a perfectly natural manner, as though he knew nothing about the affair beyond that which the priest had said to him.

" You mean to say you know

nothing about it? Why, the
whole village is full of it already!"
continued the *bátioushka*, as though
he really believed in Artem's de-
claration of ignorance concerning
the affair.

" No, I declare I know nothing
of it. If you doubt me, I'll swear
to you that it's true " (Artem
crossed himself), "and may I never
move from this spot if I lie ! "

Artem was naturally of a pious
disposition, and he only had re-
course to the above adjuration,
being convinced of the priest's
insincerity. On the other hand,
the *bátioushka*, notwithstanding
his servant's solemn oath, did not
believe a word he said.

"How should I know about
it ? " continued Artem. " I was
occupied with my work, and had
no time for gossip, or listening to
what was going on ; . . . but ask
Matrióna, if you doubt me, she
was there too ! " With these
words he turned his eyes towards
Matrióna, who was at that minute
entering the room bringing bread

and pickled cucumbers for *za-koushka*.[1] Matrióna looked at the *bátioushka* with an inquiring air.

" Have you heard tell anything about the squire's labourers, Matrióna ? " said Artem, turning to her.

" I ? What do you mean by talking like this to me ? and before the *bátioushka* too ! What should I know about them in-deed ? As if I had anything to do with the squire's labourers ! " and with this, Matrióna bounced out of the room, banging the door with unnecessary violence. "Well done ! Clever girl ! She hum-bugged him beautifully," thought Artem.

" I dare say you are quite right ! " said the *bátioushka*, wav-ing his hand. " I sent for you to wish you good luck with the hay-making. . . . I always do this, it's a custom of mine. It's a hard time now for the working man, and he needs to strengthen himself ! "

---

[1] Light refreshment.

"My respectful thanks to you, *bátioushka!*" said Artem, bowing his head. "But you know that we always have to be after some job, and never get any resting time; . . . it's never amiss to fortify oneself."

"Certainly, . . . certainly; just what I always say, and I always give orders to that effect! But you know the *matóushka* forgets! . . . The labourer certainly has a right to rest! . . . Well, have a drink."

The *bátioushka* then handed Artem a glass of *vodka,* and the latter, taking it, crossed himself, and muttered, "To your good health," drank it off, and took a slice of cucumber. He then bowed, and turned towards the door, considering the interview ended.

"Oh, stop a minute, I just want to say a word to you!" said the *bátioushka.* "It has come to my ears, (and here the *bátioushka* placed his hand on Artem's shoulder, and lowered the tone of his voice as though afraid that he might be over-heard), "it has come to my ears that you were sent out to work very early this morning. . . . This was a mistake. . . . The clock is wrong" (at this the *bátioushka* pointed reproachfully at the clock), "that's how it happened! . . . but I have given strict orders that such a thing should not happen again. You quite understand that it was all a mistake owing to the clock, and that I am very much annoyed about it, and will see that it never occurs again. Now go and get your supper, and the Lord be with you!" The priest then gave Artem his blessing.

When Artem was gone, Father Leo felt a bit happier. He had now accomplished all his duty, and clearly had earned a good rest. But before indulging in this, he repaired to his wife's bedroom to learn from her whether she approved of the manner in which he had played his part.

"Well, I don't think I said ..
too much to him, do you? No
I think it's all right?" said he,
with a slight shade of doubt in
his voice.

"Oh, I dare say you did it all
right!" condescendingly rejoined
the *matóushka*; and Father Leo,
rejoiced by this qualified ap-
proval, retired to have a good
sleep, firmly convinced that he
had that day acquitted himself
like a man.

Artem, in the meanwhile, had
gone to have his supper. The
kitchen was situated somewhat
apart from the rest of the house.
It was really nothing more or
less than an ordinary peasant's
hut, built of mud, thatched with
rushes, and having for windows
tiny square holes, fitted with bits
of green glass. Some of the
panes were broken, and had been
replaced by bits of the blue paper
in which sugar loaves are wrapped, stuck over the holes in the
glass. The *matóushka* used to
attribute reason of this makeshift

arrangement to the fact that there was no glazier in the village, although nothing in the world would have been simpler than to order panes of glass to be sent by the postmaster, who drove to the town and back once a week. Owing to this circumstance, the kitchen was in a chronic state of storm, notwithstanding the great consumption of fuel there, and atmospheric changes influenced the dwellers in it in much the same way as it did the mercury in the barometer. The cook never took off her sheepskin coat the whole winter through, and during the performance of her duties used to dance about in order to keep her feet warm. An enormous stove with a hearthstone stood in one corner of the room. Shelves were arranged along the walls, and on one side of the room was a long table, upon which meat and cabbages were chopped up, dumplings were made, &c., besides being used as a dinner table for the

servants.   A large eikon hung
in one corner ; it represented a
group of saints whose identity
was somewhat doubtful.   The
only objects clearly distinguish-
able about the picture were
bishops' mitres, and arms up-
raised in the act of giving the
blessing—these objects stood out
somewhat in relief; the rest was
entirely effaced by the action of
time, which respects nothing.   A
cord was stretched across the
kitchen, upon which the kitchen
cloths, and articles of wearing
apparel belonging to the cook
Marfa, were hanging in pic-
turesque confusion.   In order to
cross the hut it was necessary to
dip one's head in order to avoid
the risk of coming in contact
with a wet rag.   Marfa, the cook,
was a woman who had already
grown out of her first youth, but
who still retained all her strength
and vigour.   The fundamental
principles of her philosophy consisted in working as hard as ever
she could, and in replying to any

unpleasant remarks made to her with compound interest. She worked like an ox, and was as quarrelsome as a street dog, and moreover, she addressed the *matóushka* with no more respect than any one else. The latter having found that Marfa was not to be intimidated, left her alone, and so affairs went somewhat more smoothly in the kitchen than in the other departments.

Artem, on entering the kitchen, was agreeably surprised on seeing steaming hot buckwheat dumplings on the table instead of the usual herring and pickled cucumber. These dumplings were giving forth a savoury odour which appeals to the olfactory nerves of a hungry little Russian more powerfully than the most delicate aromatic balm.

"Ah, dumplings!" said Artem with an air of satisfaction. "We only want sour cream now! It wouldn't be bad, would it?"

"Yes, that's what we want!" interrupted Marfa, who had been

informed of all the recent events by Matrióna; "you send Matrióna to the *matóushka* and tell her that Artem wants sour cream."

" She'll never give it ! "

" Yes she will! She'll give you anything just now, so you had better get what you can out of her."

" All right, I'll go, if it's only for the joke of the thing. Won't she be frantic ! I expect she'll kick me out of the room ! " said Matrióna, in a jovial tone of voice, as she ran off to ask for the sour cream. Five minutes later, basins with sour cream in them were standing on the table, and with such regal fare, the *matóushka's* servants hardly knew themselves. Some one hinted that the mistress must have gone out of her mind; the dumplings and cream were nevertheless eaten with great relish.

" Well, even if it's for the last time, we shall have a good recollection of it ! " muttered Artem, wiping his mouth with his shirt-sleeve.

" Do you mean that you are going to-morrow ? " asked Marfa, in a low tone of voice.

" Why should I stay here? For the dumplings, eh ? Dumplings are well enough in their way, but I don't care enough about them for that ! I can't afford to waste time ! Every day now is worth a rouble and a half, and I am only getting ten copecks—that's just the difference. . . . "

" Artem boy! as you go through the village to-morrow, look in at my father's and tell him to come and fetch me away from here as quick as possible. Say I'll earn some money for him," said Matrióna.

" I'm not quite sure what's the best for me to do ! " rejoined Marfa with a sigh. "At my age " (she was nearly fifty), " I should hardly think they would take me on haymaking ! They would say, What do you want, old woman ? "

"Oh, no! they don't stop to ask people their age just now—they take anybody, for the crop is a plentiful one and it's hands they want! Why do you hesitate? Let us all leave the old hag in the lurch to-morrow, and let her lament! Let her go mad with rage; it's what she deserves!"

V.

THE next day was a holiday. Artem got up early as usual, and set to work to clean the horses. On this occasion he took special delight in the performance of this operation. He stroked their backs methodically and fondly, all the while making them a farewell speech which he delivered in a fragmentary sort of manner. His address was to the effect that he was cleaning them for the last time, having resolved to forsake them, and that it was scarcely to be expected that the next servant would care for them and pet them in the way that he did; that although he hated the old hag and all her belongings, a special exception was made in their case, and that he always would remain

true to them.   In fact he said the
sort of things that one says to a
friend when bidding him farewell,
and the horses evidently understood him thoroughly, for they
stood quite still, only every now
and then whisking their tails into
Artem's face in token of their
gratitude to him.

Meanwhile the sun rose from
out of the waters, and almost
instantaneously covered the
mirror-like surface of the lake
with its glory, which was simultaneously reflected by countless
myriads of dew-drops scattered
over the grass and the boughs of
trees.   Its appearance was wel-
comed by everything endowed
with consciousness of existence;
a flight of crows, by their incessant cawing in its honour,
managed to drown the feebler
choruses chanted by the sparrows, quails, and skylarks.   It
peeped into the stable at Artem,
and compelled him to put down
his curry-brush and scratch the
back of his head.

"Ah, time is getting on; I must be off!" muttered he, as he looked through the open door to see if the sun was well up. He then put on his overcoat, again scratched his head, and muttered to himself, "I feel ashamed to be seen by any one in this old coat! I really deserve a better one. . . . May *you* in the world to come be condemned to go about in such a coat!"

At this very moment the *matóushka*, who was restlessly tossing about under the bed-clothes, had spasms,[1] which almost led to the supposition that Artem's ejaculation referred to her. Poor Agraféna Ivanovna had passed a very disturbed night. She had scarcely slept at all. Thanks to her power of observation and experience, she had almost foreseen the troubles that were to overtake her on the coming day, and visions of ever-increasing expenses rose

---

[1] A popular saying in Russia, "I have spasms," *i.e.*, "Some one is talking about me."

up before her horror-stricken imagination.

The *matóushka's* wrath had, strange to say, been chiefly directed against herself. She could not forgive herself for the grand mistake she had made in her management of affairs, a mistake which certainly did not do credit to her talent for diplomacy : this was that she had omitted to draw up contracts when engaging her domestics. Had she availed herself of such contracts, she could have regarded them as her sacred property, and none of them would have even thought of leaving her service at such a critical period. But the real fact was that at that time she looked at things somewhat differently. At that time she had not considered the likelihood of a plentiful harvest ; she did not care to bind herself with contracts, so that she might have the power of sending all her servants to the right-about at any moment that

it pleased her to do so. And now
. . . that was what was causing
her such annoyance, and one
might safely answer for it that
never again would she omit any
contingencies, however remote,
from her calculations, not even
the possibility of a plentiful
harvest. Harassed by such
grievous thoughts, she tossed
about all night, and only towards
morning, when thoroughly exhausted, did she manage to get
off to sleep. But it would have
been better had she not slept.
She dreamed that every one had
left her service, and that no one
was willing to work for her. She
entreated, promised large sums
of money, but all in vain. The
thick, full-eared rye had ripened
on her land; meanwhile the
pitiless sun was pouring out its
rays upon the ears, so that the
grain was falling out of them.
All this wealth was vanishing
before her very eyes, and every
one absolutely refused to help
her. " This must be because I

am so wicked," thought she, and began to call for her husband to come and help her. But Father Leo was sleeping the sleep of the just. To look at him one would think he would never wake again. Agraféna Ivanovna, seized with a sudden terror, awaked from her sleep. Things were still not quite so bad in reality, thank God. But it was time to get up, for the sun was rising. It was an unheard-of thing that the *matóushka* should stay in bed after the sun had risen. She dressed herself, and hurried out into the yard to ascertain whether Marfa had fed the ducks and geese. She met Artem in the yard.

"Where are you off to so early?" thought the *matóushka* to herself in trepidation.

"I've got to go into the village," began Artem, coming up to her, and taking off his hat.

"What for?" inquired the *matóushka*, fixing her scrutinising gaze upon him.

" Oh, I want to see my family !
To-day is a holiday, you know ! "
replied Artem.

The *matóushka* turned round,
and went away without saying
anything.

Artem left the yard, but instead of going to see his family
he turned off in precisely the
opposite direction. Three houses
away from the priest's, on the
left-hand side, the squire's estate
office was situated.

It consisted of a couple of
large huts, one of which was
occupied by the bailiff and his
family ; the other, resembling in
appearance an ordinary shed,
was used as a workmen's kitchen,
and night shelter for them in
bad weather. Adjacent to these
buildings was an enormous yard
blocked up with reaping and
threshing machines, waggon
wheels, axles, and other separate
portions of carts. At the further
end of the yard was a smith's
forge—a small mud hut, roofed
with black earth, on which vari-

ous kinds of weeds were sprouting. Artem went straight up to one of the bailiffs. Near by, a crowd of labourers were waiting to receive their week's wages. Seated behind a high counter was the bailiff with the closely-cropped whiskers, known as the "cunning dog." Rapidly balancing each man's account, he handed him an order for the sum due. Artem, after awaiting his turn, entered the office.

"What do you want?" asked the bailiff, eyeing him from top to toe.

"I come for a job!" replied Artem, in a tone of assurance.

"A job! Hm! What do you mean by coming here for a job when you are engaged with the *bátioushka*?"

"Oh, I've settled up with the *bátioushka*!"

"I dare say. More likely that you've got wind that wages are high now, and without any more ado you have left your master. Ah, you fellows! it's a taste of the knout that you want! Where's your passport?"

The "cunning dog" had guessed aright. It should be remarked that this bailiff was on very friendly terms with Father Leo and his wife. Two years previously he had married a young woman who, strange to relate, had contrived to remain nearly four years at a stretch in the *matóushka's* service, and ever since that time the bailiff Matveï had never missed taking tea with the *matóushka* every Sunday, and used constantly to assure her that she was his benefactress. Yesterday he had gone straight from the fields to the priest's house in order to inform her of the startling events which had happened. It was then settled that in case either Artem or the other two servants should come and offer their services to the squire, their application should be refused, and that they should be turned out of the office without ceremony.

Artem hesitated somewhat when asked for his passport, and answered with a certain amount of confusion that the *bátioushka* still had it.

"Well, we don't take stray adventurers without passports! What do you want?" said he, suddenly addressing himself to another man, who was awaiting his turn, thus clearly showing that he did not intend to waste any more words with Artem.

Artem left the office with his head hanging down. But he had not lost courage yet, and there was still a good chance of success. After all, the squire's estate was not the only one in the world. He had quite resolved that, come what might, he no longer intended to bow and scrape before the *matóushka;* and more than that, even if she went on her knees before him, he would no longer remain in her service. "But supposing . . .," and then an unpleasant reflection entered Artem's head.

What would happen if he met with a similar reception wherever he applied for work? And worse than that might happen—for, having no passport, he was liable to find himself locked up in a cool cell during this scorching weather, and thus not only earn nothing, but lose all that was due to him for his winter's work into the bargain.

"Artem Maximovitch!" cried a familiar voice to him, as he stepped out of the office door.

"Ah, that's you, Teréshko!" rejoined Artem, looking up and seeing before him a tall, sturdy peasant, in his best white blouse and a black sheepskin hat. Teréshko was about forty years old, but his long beard was already streaked with grey hairs, and when he lifted his cap it could be seen that he was bald. This man was Matrióna's father, a man known to the whole village for his extraordinary strength and desperate poverty. The latter misfortune might

16

perhaps be accounted for by
Teréshko's fondness for strong
drink, and Artem was somewhat
surprised at seeing him sober on
a holiday.

"Why, Teréshko, how's 'this
that to-day you are not . . .?"

"Not drunk?" interrupted
Teréshko.

"Well, yes! It seems strange,
somehow!"

"Ha, ha! Well, it would not
do to-day! I mustn't go to the
public-house: it won't do to lose
this fine weather; I must get to
work! I have got nothing left
at all at home; they tell me I've
drunk it all, but upon my word
there never was much there to
drink. And now, you see, I have
gone in for a new suit: things are
looking up with us now!" And
Teréshko complacently twirled
his moustaches, which were truly
of Cossack dimensions. "But
what I wanted to ask you is
whether you have come here for
a job?"

"Well, what if I have?"

"What made you go to that rogue for a job: he's a mercenary dog of a fellow! Why, don't you know that he is ready to lick the *matóushka's* shoes? You had far better go to the office at Kousmínski: they will take you on there without asking any questions, because they are short of hands, and they are anxious enough to find any of our fellows to take a job. I am working for them myself, so we may as well go down there together. It's not more than a short five versts from here. Ah, Artem Maximovitch, this is a wonderful time we are having now, I tell you the truth. I've lived forty-two years on the earth, and have never seen the like of it before. There will be some profit for our fellows at last! Truly God has at last had pity on them."

Artem accepted Teréshko's proposal without much hesitation. He then delivered Matrióna's message.

"Ha, ha! My Matrióna is a sharp girl!" remarked Teréshko, in a tone expressive of satisfaction. "I've thought before now of taking her away. Why should she slave away there for nothing? I shall take her off to-morrow to Kousminski to get her a job. She will get work at raking up the hay. She is a first-rate hand at that."

To judge by Teréshko's remarks about his daughter, one could see that she occupied a big place in her father's heart. This was easy to understand, for she was his only surviving daughter, her sisters having all been carried off one unlucky winter by an epidemic of diphtheria.

It was about noon when Artem, having visited his wife and children, returned to his post.

"It's dinner-time!" exclaimed Marfa to him, as he entered the yard gate.

"It's not time," rejoined

Artem, with a preoccupied air. "Where are the *bátioushka* and *matóushka* ?"

The priest and his wife were in the sitting-room, and Artem repaired thither unannounced. When he appeared the *matóushka* hastily disappeared, so that he only caught sight of her retreating figure as he entered. Father Leo, this time arrayed in his ordinary coat, was just sitting down to dinner. Before him was set out a decanter of *vodka* and a dish of herrings, prepared by Argraféna Ivanovna herself.

"Ah, that's right, Artem Maximovitch!" exclaimed the priest in a very friendly manner. "I like to see you come of your own accord before dinner; you must look after yourself a little, you know! If you had only done this before, there would have always been a glass ready for you!"

Saying this, Father Leo began to pour out a glass of *vodka*, evidently intended for Artem.

"Thank you kindly; only I have not come for that."

"Well, what have you come for?"

"To settle up my account! I humbly pray you to reckon up my wages due!"

This answer completely took the *bátioushka* by surprise, and for a moment he had no reply ready to hand. This caused him to reflect for a couple of minutes, an act which cost him no small effort.

"But look here! have you any cause for dissatisfaction?"

This question provoked an almost imperceptible smile on Artem's features. It seemed strange that it should be necessary for the *bátioushka* to ask such a question.

"Oh no . . . that is to say, not in particular. . . . But you know every one has to look out for himself. . . . "

"Well, of course I don't deny the truth of that," said Father Leo, in a conciliatory manner;

"but still, my friend, you must surely have some good reason for what you are doing! Listen to me, Artem Maximovitch; we will be plain with one another— I, as the pastor, as the good pastor, and you as the spiritual son, as the obedient spiritual son! . . ."

With these words Father Leo got up, approached Artem, and laid his hand on his shoulder— an action usually resorted to by this good pastor in his friendly admonition of the parishioners.

"We will be plain with one another!" continued he in a voice now becoming pathetic and even tremulous with emotion— "I will not dispute the fact that you have been uncomfortable in my service. I can see it myself now, but it was really an oversight. . . . You know the *matóushka* seems to be exacting, but she is really a good soul! You know how I am situated; she has to look after everything herself, and this is really impossible for one person; . . . but in future I intend to take care and see for myself that the servants are well looked after. And there is another thing I have to say to you. We are not wild beasts, we are human beings after all. . , . I admit that I think your salary is low. According to the winter scale of prices it is perhaps not too low. Work is light in winter, and is, to a great extent, indoors ; . . . but now, I admit, things are different, and I offer to increase your pay. . . . I will give you ninety roubles instead of forty. . . . So you see that, after all, we do think a little about your interests. . . . "

"I thank you sincerely, *bátioushka*, but nevertheless I must ask you to settle up with me. I am afraid that I cannot possibly accept your offer. . . . " And Artem bowed low to the priest.

At this moment the door opened and Teréshko entered. His first action was to cross himself in front of the *icon* (Teréshko was a devout man), and he then bowed to Father Leo.

"Good day, Terénti! What brings you here?"

"At your service, sir!" replied Teréshko, in a quiet manner. "I've come to fetch my daughter, so will you kindly settle up her account with me?"

Father Leo was thoroughly nonplussed this time. He was beginning to feel bored by all this business; he felt quite weak and tired, and was longing to get back to bed again. He was not a man of ready wit, and had no sort of idea of getting himself out of a difficult situation. At this moment, however, assistance of an unexpected nature arrived: the door leading out of the sitting-room was burst open, and Agraféna Ivanovna impulsively rushed in. One could foretell by her purple countenance, and her eyeballs rolling about, that a storm was brewing, and that her pent-up wrath must ere long burst

forth. It was equally obvious
that she must have been standing behind this same door during
the above described conversation, and that she had overheard
everything.

" No!" she thundered forth in
a terrifying voice. " This is
more than I can stand. I have
endured and suffered long enough;
this is too much! What's the
meaning of this? You've been
conspiring, have you? *Canaille*,
brigands, rogues, cut-throats!
O-o-o! I can't stand it any
longer. You want to be paid
off?—Money given you?—Your
passports handed back? Is that
so? Perhaps you don't want
them? No? You don't!"—(at
this the *matóushka* snapped her
fingers contemptuously)—"Clear
out this minute! What are you
standing there for? Be off with
you, I say! Collect your goods
and chattels, your beggarly rags,
and don't let me catch sight of
you again!"

Teréshko and Artem thought

it best to clear out while they
could do so with a whole skin,
and the *matoúshka* accompanied
them beyond the yard gates, all
the while giving vent to her
feelings with violent words. Her
classic words were audible for
fully five hundred yards around.
At the sound of her voice some
of the more curious of the people
came together to hear her and
admire this edifying scene, and
the female part of the assembly,
whose tongues never tire of wag-
ging, made biting remarks: "How
abusive she is!"   "She's not in
our style!" or else, "Take a
lesson from her, women, if you
wish to learn how to swear
properly!" The *matoúshka* sur-
passed herself on this occasion.
She expressed wishes that never
were likely to be realised—as, for
instance, that Artem with his
whole family, his hut, and even
his dogs and calves (which un-
fortunately he did not possess),
might sink into the earth ; she
even invoked the blameless shade

of the late Maxim Klad'ko in heaven, wishing that he might turn in his grave seven times. Concerning Teréshko, she prayed that he, his children and belongings might be utterly consumed and return to ashes. Finally, the *matóushka* having exhausted all the expressions at her disposal, expressed a wish that the earth might open and swallow up Kramariévka.

Fortunately this petition remains unanswered.

On the following day our heroes were hard at work in the fields. At the *Kousmínski* office no unpleasant questions had been asked about passports, &c., for they had no reason for so doing, besides which it was not the time to bother about passports, especially as the applicants were well known to the other labourers. Teréshko and Artem, wielding their scythes in magnificent style, worked in the foremost rank of the reapers: Matrióna was sustaining her

reputation in the raking depart-
ment, to the delight of her admiring parent, Teréshko. Close
by was Marfa, working with her
might and main not to be left
behind : the bitter experience
of solitude in the *matóushka's*
kitchen had proved too much for
her, and so she had quietly collected her belongings, consisting
of a few wretched worn-out rags
given her by her mistress when
in one of her "tenderer moods,"
and, unobserved by any one,
had slipped out of the priest's
house.

From the eastern side of the
sky the ,morning sun poured
out its gladdening rays ; the
fresh morning breeze whistled
joyously, fondly caressing the
silken tops of the luxuriant grass
which covered the level, boundless steppe ; the larks warbled
cheerfully, the sparrows twittered
. . . and our heroes looked gladly
on this scene of abundance sent
by God, with the feelings experienced by those who find

themselves at liberty again on a bright sunny spring day, after long years of grievous imprisonment.

THE END.

UNWIN BROS., PRINTERS CHILWORTH AND LONDON.

Unwin's Novel Series.

Pocket size, 6½ inches by 4½ inches.

In stiff paper wrapper, price 1s. 6d. each.

"The rivalry with Tauchnitz is not to be single-handed. Mr. Fisher Unwin has made arrangements for introducing the volumes of his Novel Series—*the* 'English Tauchnitz,' *as we called it at the time—to the Continental and Colonial bookselling trade. The series will not be confined to fiction, but will include popular biographies, works in general literature, and books of travel."*—Pall Mall Gazette.

"'Tauchnitz has a formidable rival in Paternoster Square. We mean Mr. Fisher Unwin, whose **Novel Series** is sure to become universally popular. In handiness of form and tastefulness of binding and beauty of printing, **Unwin's Novel Series** stands alone."—*Echo.*

"Both the type and the paper are better, but the size is precisely the same as the handy and popular Tauchnitz volumes."—*Leeds Mercury.*

1. **GLADY'S FANE : A Story** of Two Lives. By T. WEMYSS REID, Author of "Life of Rt. Hon. W. E. Forster."

2. **ISAAC ELLER'S MONEY.** By Mrs. ANDREW DEAN, Author of "A Splendid Cousin."

3. **CONCERNING OLIVER KNOX.** By G. COLMORE, Author of "The Conspiracy of Silence."

OTHER VOLUMES IN PREPARATION.

The Illustrated Cover forms a special feature of the NOVEL SERIES, the Publisher having invited prominent artists to contribute to each Novel their ideal of the heroine of the story.

LONDON :
T. FISHER UNWIN, PATERNOSTER SQUARE, E.C.

www.ingramcontent.com/pod-product-compliance
Lightning Source LLC
Chambersburg PA
CBHW031426020726
47499CB00005B/1610